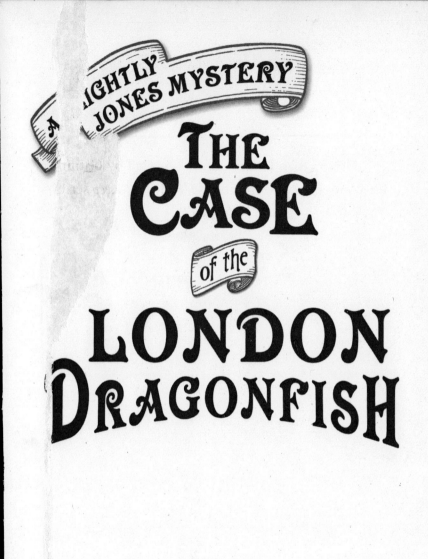

A KNIGHTLY JONES MYSTERY

THE CASE *of the*

LONDON DRAGONFISH

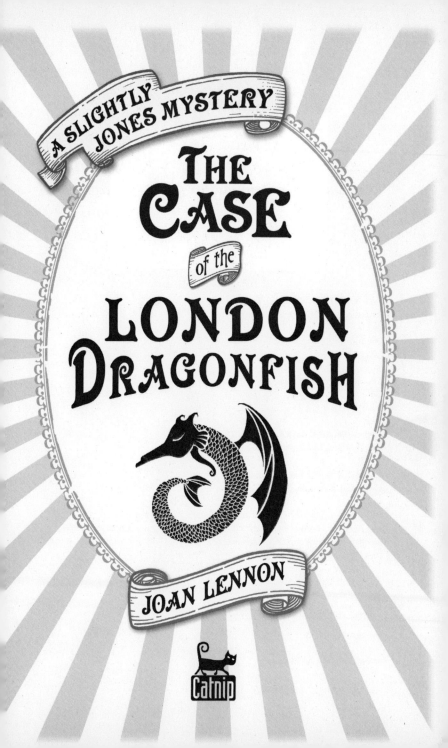

A SLIGHTLY JONES MYSTERY

THE CASE

of the

LONDON DRAGONFISH

JOAN LENNON

Catnip

CATNIP BOOKS
Published by Catnip Publishing Ltd
14 Greville Street
London
EC1N 8SB

This edition first published 2010

1 3 5 7 9 10 8 6 4 2

Cover design by Mandy Norman
Cover illustration by Shane Clester

A CIP catalogue record for this book is available from the British Library.

ISBN 978-1-84647-098-1

Printed in Poland

www.catnippublishing.co.uk

Everybody's heard of Florence Nightingale
and David Livingstone. These books are dedicated
to the Victorian heroes and heroines
who aren't quite so famous!

This one is for
Mary Anning – Fossil Finder

CONTENTS

CHAPTER ONE:
Shadow in the Dark

The night-watchman's footsteps echoed in the darkness. He was carrying a lantern, but it had no chance of lighting more than a tiny circle of the enormous black space through which he moved. Emptiness arched above him, high as a cathedral. Dim shapes loomed as the man paced past: skeletons and skulls, animal heads, and gigantic bodies covered with fur, scales, rough hide.

What sort of nightmare place would house such horrors?

But the man showed no fear. Granted, he was mumbling to

himself, but it was just that − mumbling. He wasn't whimpering or gibbering, which would make more sense given the ghastly glints of giant teeth and razor claws to be glimpsed on either side of him. He was just talking to himself in a preoccupied but perfectly calm way.

'Perhaps it would be better if the blood-stained letter is first discovered in Chapter Three? *Before* Lord Algernon is accused of the murder? I wonder . . . That might very well be the answer! And then I could . . .'

For a moment it was almost as if the grisly monstrosities were leaning closer out of the shadows, trying to catch his words − if so, they were out of luck. The rest of the watchman's muttering was lost as he and his circle of lantern light passed under the far archway and disappeared into another part of the building. The echo of his boots could still be heard, but then that too died away. The threatening shapes retreated into the dark once more. For a long time, nothing disturbed the stillness − not a breath of air, not a murmur, not a sigh.

Then part of a shadow detached itself and ran across the floor.

The scratch of a sulphur match seemed louder than an explosion. As a dark-lantern was lit and the door quickly shut, the brief flare seared the darkness like a flash of lightning. Tiny muffled clattering noises made small dents in the silence – there was a screech of hinges – another scurrying of feet across the stone floor – and then . . .

Nothing.

CHAPTER TWO:
Hammering at the Door

'**S**lightly!' called Granny Tonic. 'Wake up!'

Slightly Jones groaned and rolled over. She'd stayed up far too late last night reading the adventures of the famous detective, Mr Sherlock Holmes, until her candle guttered and went out. (Since her bedroom was at the top of the house, it would be a while before a gaslight was fitted.) Slightly read everything she could get her hands on about the great man because she was determined to become a detective herself when she grew up. If not sooner . . .

'Slightly!'

Detectives never sleep in, Slightly told herself firmly, and got out of bed. She looked in the mirror on the off-chance that her appearance had somehow magically changed in the night. It hadn't. She still didn't look like a detective. She still just looked like a girl – skinny and freckly and small, with hateful red hair and a pointy little face like an inquisitive ferret.

Slightly sighed. She threw on her clothes, splashed water on her face, stuck her tongue out at her reflection and clattered halfway down the stairs. Then she turned around and raced back to collect her detecting notebook and the silver propelling pencil Granny had given her for her last birthday.

'Good morning, Granny,' she said, bouncing into the kitchen.

In fact, Granny Tonic was Slightly's mother's aunt, so technically she was her Great-Aunt and not her Granny, but since *everybody* called her Granny, Slightly did too. She had come to Granny's house when she was a baby, after the death of her parents. Because she couldn't remember her father or mother, she didn't miss them, except in a wondering what-if sort of way. Besides, Granny and the boarders of Limpopo House gave her plenty of family to be going on with.

Slightly knew that Limpopo was a river in South Africa but why Granny had named her house that was a mystery. It was just one hint among many that Granny had led a *very* interesting life, but whenever Slightly asked her about it, she always said,

'That's a long story.'

'But I love long stories!' Slightly would cry.

'Well, then, I shall have to tell you some day.'

And not a word more would Slightly get out of her.

But today Slightly wasn't thinking about anybody's distant and tantalising past.

'Good morning, Slightly,' said Granny. 'And what day are we on?'

'Day Three!' said Slightly proudly. 'I haven't lost my temper since Friday and here we are, bright and shiny, on Monday! I think I'll go for a whole *week* this time.'

'We'll see,' said Granny.

The autumn sunshine streamed into the basement kitchen. Granny Tonic always kept the back door open whenever the weather allowed, to let in the light and the air.

'I'm always at home to fresh air.' That's what Granny said.

Everyone at Limpopo House ate their meals at the big oak table, now that the dining room had become Mr Reginald Westerly's room. It had the best light and, as all artists know, a good light is half the battle. He was the newest of the boarders, and Slightly loved his magnificent moustache (even though she suspected he dyed it that wonderful black) and the way he always treated her as if she were a proper grown-up (even though she wasn't).

No one really minded eating in the kitchen. It was more convenient for Granny and more friendly. (Miss Sally Forth, their only lady boarder, fluttered a bit about it being not quite respectable. But since it meant Cleopatra, her elderly cat, had quick and easy access to the garden when required, she didn't actually mean it.)

So far this morning only Mr Malcolm Gentler (first floor front room) had come down for breakfast, so he was helping Granny Tonic and Slightly get things ready for the others.

'I'm desperate to know what Mr Thurgood came up with last night. He said he was going to work on "Chapter Four: The Mystery of the Blood-stained Letter"! Don't you love that title, Mr Gentler?' asked Slightly as she set a pile of toast in front of him.

'I do – it's very trembly violins, don't you think?' said Mr Gentler in his soft Scottish voice as he buttered the toast. He was a young-ish man. Slightly thought he was probably older than Mr Thurgood but not as old as Mr Westerly. He was a musician, and he buttered toast the way he did everything – in time to the music inside his head. This meant that some people's toast swam in butter and other people's had less than a scrape, but no one dreamt of complaining.

'Spooky!' said Slightly Jones as she passed Granny a bowl of eggs from the pantry. 'He said he was determined to figure out whose blood it was on that letter. So far it's been a complete mystery.' Mr Thurgood was writing a detective novel. It had no title yet, but it was *very* exciting.

'Don't worry. If Mr Thurgood can't come up with an answer, I'm sure you will,' said Mr Gentler, smiling serenely and dripping butter onto his waistcoat.

Granny rattled a shovelful of coal into the range. 'Careful, Mr Gentler,' she warned. 'Not too much buttering up in my house or you'll make the girl proud!'

Mr Gentler may have been a bit messy, but he was completely right about Slightly. Mr Thurgood was really excellent at imagining mystifying crimes, puzzling clues and false trails. Unfortunately, he wasn't quite so good at imagining answers and solutions. Detective-in-training Slightly had helped him out of more than one fictional predicament.

Nevertheless,

'One day the name of Thurgood will be as well known to the reading public as that of Mr Dickens or Miss Austen,' was what Granny Tonic always said, and Slightly believed her. Every morning she waited eagerly at the breakfast table for Mr Thurgood to come home and tell them what his characters had been up to that night. And not just her! They all did – Mr Gentler, Mr Westerly, even Miss Forth who pretended to think that popular fiction was really too vulgar for her delicate tastes, but still made sure she never missed a word.

Mr Thurgood had been the first boarder to come to stay at Granny Tonic's house. Everyone who came to stay at Limpopo House was special.

'I'm always at home to interesting people.' That's what Granny said.

Mr Thurgood, for example, was a writer with a problem. He had struggled for years with not being able to sleep at night. He couldn't get a wink of shut-eye all through the dark hours and then he was too sleepy to do any writing – or work of any sort – when the sun came up. It was Granny Tonic who realised the solution to his problem.

'What you need is a job that happens at night – when you're awake – but one that will also leave you with plenty of freedom in which to write,' she'd said firmly. 'What you need is a job as a night-watchman. And I think I know just the place . . .'

The place Granny had in mind turned out to be the Natural History Museum!

Slightly couldn't think of anywhere more thrilling. Of all the wonderful new London museums and galleries, she loved the Natural History Museum the best. She went all goosebumpy every time she'd been there for a visit. And it wasn't just the creatures and fossils and exhibits that were so wonderful (though they were!). It was the great big blue and beige building itself, and especially the terracotta decorations – the weird pterodactyls and wolf-like beasts that guarded the outside, the evil-looking monkeys and scary deep-sea fish inside. She had two special favourites: the kangaroo over the great front doors and the bat-eared foxes by the main stairs. (She used to think *they* were particularly fond of *her* as well, but she was too old for silliness like that now.)

'Could Mr Thurgood really get a job there?' Slightly had asked.

'I've known one of the Professors there since we were children – Professor Appleword,' Granny had replied. 'I will write to him immediately . . .'

And the very next day, Mr Thurgood, his clothes freshly pressed and his hair slicked down with

Macassar oil, went right up to the big double doors of the Natural History Museum and offered his services as night-watchman. From that day to this, he had been a happy man and an even happier novelist. He was never lonely. Even in the dead of night, walking up and down the galleries without another living soul to speak to, his head was full of characters, events, mysteries and chapter headings.

'Oh, good morning!' fluted Miss Forth as she rustled into the kitchen. Slightly looked at her, then down at herself and sighed. No matter how late Miss Forth had stayed up, working at her translating (for her skill at languages was how she made her living) she was always beautifully groomed the next morning.

Slightly had asked Granny once how old Miss Forth was, partly because she was curious and partly because she wondered if perhaps just growing up helped you look neater. Granny had said, 'She's old enough not to be asked.' When Slightly had asked what that meant, Granny replied, 'Usually it means about 30.'

'Where is Mr Westerly? And, er, Mr Thurgood?' Miss Forth was asking now.

'Is our soon-to-be-famous author not back yet?' asked Mr Westerly as he also appeared. His magnificent moustache shone in the sunlight, the ends waxed up into fierce little smiles on either side of his nose. (It was possible to tell just how well one of Mr Westerly's paintings was going by the state of his moustache – this morning, his work was obviously going very well indeed.)

Before Slightly could answer, there was the sound of the front door opening and closing, followed by a cheerful whistling along the corridor.

'Good morning, everyone!' said Mr Thurgood as he came in. 'And a good morning it is!'

'You don't mean . . .' said Slightly, trying not to spill the tea in her excitement, 'you don't mean you've cracked it?! You've discovered whose blood it is on the mysterious letter?'

'Ah!' crowed Mr Thurgood, looking thoroughly delighted with himself. 'I'm glad you asked – just listen to *this*!' And he pulled up a chair, took a quick slurp of tea and was just about to tell them all about it – when there was a great thundering and hammering at the front door. It sounded to Slightly as if a small army was beating on it with heavy sticks. Whoever it was very much wanted *in*.

'Heavens, who can that be?' said Granny, taking off her apron and smoothing her hair. 'They'll be having the paint off if they're not careful!'

She swept out of the room. The pounding continued. Everybody eavesdropped shamelessly as she flung open the front door and demanded to know what all the ruckus was about.

'Out of my way, my good woman!' demanded a voice no one recognised. 'We know he's in here!'

'What do you –' they heard Granny squawk and then three large policemen in high-collared tunics and helmets burst into the kitchen, waving their sticks menacingly.

'That's him!' cried one. 'That's the thief! Grab him!'

To Slightly's horror and amazement they threw themselves bodily at Mr Thurgood!

Granny appeared in the kitchen doorway, her hair coming out of its pins and her face red.

'*What do you –*' she began again, but the policemen ignored her.

The biggest of them rumbled, 'We are arresting you, Earnest Thurgood, for the wilful vandalism and outright theft of a valuable exhibit from the Natural History Museum on Cromwell Road, the crime to have taken place in the early hours of this morning. And I would be very much surprised indeed if the judge does not send you to prison for a very long time.'

'*WHAT?!*' everyone exclaimed, but Mr Thurgood exclaimed the loudest of all.

'I don't know what you're talking about!' he wailed.

He looks so small! Slightly thought, as the enormous policemen loomed over him, holding Mr Thurgood's arms as if he were some dangerous animal that might bite at any moment.

It made her heart hurt.

'You heard me,' said the biggest policeman roughly. 'Wasn't nobody else there, and didn't nobody else break in – we checked. The lock on the exhibit case has been picked and the Chinese box the fossil was supposed to be in is empty. We don't need to go searching for suspects. It was you, all right. You're coming with us!'

Pandemonium broke out. Granny shouted, Miss Forth shrieked (and pretended to swoon), Mr Gentler waved the butter knife about in an agitated double time, Mr Westerly bellowed and tried to detach the men from Mr Thurgood by poking them vigorously in the ribs and bristling his moustache. Slightly kicked one of the policemen hard on the shins and tried her best to trip up one of the others, but that didn't stop them. The last thing she saw was Mr Thurgood's face, chalk white and bewildered, before he was dragged away, out of the sunny kitchen, down the corridor and into the street.

The front door slammed. An appalled silence filled the house.

Slightly felt sick. Things like this just didn't happen! Granny's was a safe, respectable household. Wasn't it?

She looked about, but there was shock and confusion on every face – no one seemed to know what to think or what to do.

'How could Mr Thurgood *do* such a thing?!' whispered Miss Forth.

'He couldn't,' insisted Slightly. 'You know perfectly *well* he couldn't!' But the last words were practically a wail.

'Oh, no, of course, oh, I didn't mean …' stammered Miss Forth. Her eyes welled up, but Granny was having none of that.

'Slightly,' she said briskly. 'Fetch my hat. I'm going out.'

Slightly wasn't sure what Granny was planning to do, but she *was* sure that she had no intention of being left out of it!

'Slightly? Hurry up, girl – I said I'm going out.'

Slightly checked that her notebook and pencil

were in her pocket. Then she drew herself up to her
full height and stuck out her chin.

'No, you're not, Granny,' she said firmly. '*We* are.'

CHAPTER THREE:
Death by Giant Sloth

As they hurried down the street, Slightly's head was buzzing. *I wonder where we're going? Are we going to rescue poor Mr Thurgood? Or interview him? What would Mr Sherlock Holmes do? We need clues. Since Mr Thurgood certainly didn't do it, who is the real thief? I need a name for this case to put in my notebook – how about 'The Curious Incident of the Novelist in the Night'?*

'Oh, *why* can you never see an omnibus when you need one?!' Granny exclaimed crossly, breaking into Slightly's thoughts. 'It's so *irritating!*'

'And when we do see one, where will we be going?' asked Slightly.

'To the Natural History Museum.'

AH! thought Slightly.

'To view the scene of the crime?' she said.

'To tell Professor Appleword that he's made a terrible mistake.'

Granny sounded fierce. Slightly had a moment's sympathy for the Professor.

Then, as they continued to look out for an omnibus, Granny turned to her and said in a low voice, 'I saw you kick that policeman, Slightly.'

Rats! thought Slightly. She'd really hoped nobody'd seen that. 'Yes, Granny. I just . . . he just . . . I lost my temper. Sorry.' Slightly knew she wasn't really sorry about kicking the policeman at all. In fact, she wished she'd kicked him harder! But she *was* sorry about losing her temper. She'd been doing so well – she'd lasted two whole days!

'Hmm,' said Granny. 'You know what . . . I don't think we'll count this one. That policeman thoroughly deserved it. Here's the omnibus, and I suggest we say no more about it.' And she waved her umbrella to get the driver to stop.

The omnibus was overcrowded, as always. Slightly ended up wedged between Granny and a lady who was either wearing a really serious corset or else had remarkably bony hips. Either way, it was very uncomfortable. But detectives often had to endure discomfort. The trick was to take your mind off it by thinking about all the facts and clues you'd collected, and put them into logical order. But Slightly didn't *have* any clues or facts yet – other than the fact that Mr Thurgood was innocent. So she thought about . . . hair.

Slightly remembered asking Granny once, 'Is it true that people with red hair lose their tempers more often than people with beautifully wavy brown hair? Or angelic blonde hair? Or hair the colour of a raven's wing?' In all the books she'd read (including Mr Thurgood's unpublished one) there were *never* any ginger lady detectives, solving problems and saving the day.

Was this because a person who loses her temper all the time would have a lot of trouble thinking clearly and solving dilemmas and predicaments? Slightly could certainly see that it would be hard to save the day if you were busy stamping your feet and screeching. So she really wanted to know if her hair was the root of her problem.

Granny hadn't been much help. They had been in the middle of preparing dinner, and she just gave

Slightly a long hard look and said, 'That pie's going to burn if you're not careful.'

Slightly had pondered on this as she pulled out the pie. (It was only a little scorched around the edges.) It was all right for Granny. Her hair was pure white, and even if it had been sky blue and purple, *nobody* would dare pass any comments. Because although Granny herself never lost her temper, she very occasionally *threatened* to and *that* was scary enough!

Granny Tonic was a formidable woman.

I wish I were formidable, Slightly had thought as she scratched off the charred bits of the crust, but somehow she couldn't imagine that would ever be true. *I'll be 183 years old and Granny will still be saying to me, 'Slightly! Think first!'*

Slightly's thoughts were proving just as uncomfortable as her seat. She looked out, but they were only just coming to the edge of Hyde Park. Even the sight of the cows grazing peacefully on the last of the summer grass didn't please her the way it usually did.

Hurry up! she thought. *Hurry up!*

When they turned the corner into Cromwell Road, however, they slowed down even more. The street was clogged with carriages and the pavement was filled with spectators. The omnibus couldn't get through.

'Seems to be a kerfuffle up ahead, ladies and gentlemen,' said the driver. 'Could be a bit of a wait.' And he got down, gave the horses their nose-bags and lit his pipe.

'Well!' exclaimed a rather ample middle-aged man who could really have done with a larger coat. '*He* certainly believes in making himself comfortable. I shall certainly complain! I certainly don't expect to sit here half the day – Madam!' This was directed at Granny who was edging past the other passengers with Slightly at her heels. 'Madam, what are you doing? You certainly can't be thinking of *walking*?!'

'I certainly can,' said Granny solemnly. Slightly snorted a giggle and then tried to pretend it was just a cough. The ample gentleman glared at them through the window and turned up his nose.

Once out on the pavement, Granny asked a white-haired woman in a shawl what the commotion was about.

'Well, Ma'am, Miss,' the woman said to them. 'The Museum should be open, but it's not. It was meant to be a Special Exhibition, see, with fossils and such all the way from China. My son's a sailor in the China Seas right now, so I came along when I heard of it.

But now they've closed the doors. I don't know why.'

She showed them one of the posters tied to the railings advertising the Exhibition, especially something called a 'Dragonfish', which was hailed as a new wonder of the age – a Missing Link.

The China Seas! thought Slightly, eyes shining. *A Dragonfish!*

'They're saying the Queen, God bless her, is to be coming to see it herself,' the woman continued. 'A special Private Viewing. I do hope it's true, the dear lady being still so sad, even after all these years, and an outing is a cheering thing for anyone, even the highest in the land! I hope you don't think me disrespectful, but I'm a widow-woman myself and I feel for her, I truly do.'

'Not in the least – your feelings do you nothing but credit,' said Granny, and Slightly agreed. Everyone in the whole country wished the Queen could be happier.

They thanked the woman and moved on. As they made their way through the crowd they heard a number of explanations for the closing of the Museum, each one wilder than the next.

'. . . and when they came to open it up this morning, all the fossils had disappeared! The whole entire building was completely empty . . .'

'. . . that's not it. I heard they'd all come to life in the night and moved themselves around and now they're all in the wrong places and the staff is busy moving them all back again . . .'

'. . . I heard there was a murder, because of the Queen maybe coming . . .'

' . . . I heard the man murdered was one of the Queen's special guards who'd come to find out if the Museum was safe for her . . .'

'. . . well, looks like he found out too, don't it?! . . .'

'. . . and I heard there was a murder and it was the Queen's special guard and his body was found *in seventeen pieces inside that great big sloth creature* . . .'

'. . . Oooh, I hate that great thing – it scares me to death and it makes little Freddy here cry every time we go to see it. We go to see the horrible great sloth every time we come to the Museum, don't we, Freddy? . . .'

'The sloth was a herbivore, Ma'am,' Slightly couldn't resist explaining as she passed.

The woman stared at her. 'Well, I don't see what religion has to do with it, little Miss,' she said huffily and turned away with a sniff.

Slightly felt her face going red and opened her mouth to put the woman right in no uncertain terms – when Granny took her by the arm and, with a quick shake of the head, led her on.

'Remember – think first, dear,' she murmured.

A dirty boy with mud-coloured hair and bright brown eyes grinned rudely at Slightly, and stuck out his tongue. Slightly stuck her tongue out right back at him.

Fortunately Granny didn't see.

CHAPTER FOUR:
He Will See Me!

Slightly was still fuming when they arrived at the ornate gates. Normally they would be open to welcome in the idly curious, the earnest amateur and the serious scientist, but not today.

'Sorry, Ma'am, Museum's closed,' said the guard wearily. He was young and a bit rumpled-looking. He obviously did not enjoy repeatedly disappointing everyone by keeping them out.

Granny smiled at him. 'Yes, I understand the giant sloth has eaten someone important. Most inconsiderate! But we're not here to visit the Museum.

We wish to speak with Professor Appleword.'

The guard shuffled his feet nervously. 'Well, I don't know, Ma'am . . . Professor Appleword's awfully busy just now . . . How about coming back another day?'

'I think not, young man. *Today* is when I wish to speak with him.' Granny's smile had disappeared, and she spoke in a voice Slightly recognised all too well. It was her 'You Will Do As I Say. Now.' voice.

The guard made one more feeble attempt.

'I . . . I'm not sure Professor Appleword is seeing *anyone* today, Ma'am, I'm really not.'

'He will see me.' The words were delivered in her dangerously quiet 'You Really Do Not Wish to Make Me Lose My Temper' voice.

Slightly watched the young guard wince. She knew just how he felt.

'No, Ma'am – I mean yes, Ma'am,' he said, fumbling with the lock. 'Come through, Ma'am. Young Miss.'

'Thank you,' said Granny. She was all kindness again, the threat of steel carefully concealed until it was needed next.

'What a pleasant young man,' she said loudly as they walked away. 'I am sure he will go far.' Slightly looked back and gave the guard a sympathetic look. He wiped his forehead and waggled his eyebrows at her.

Up the sweeping ramp to the entrance they hurried (Slightly giving the kangaroo over the door a quick greeting smile), on through the great front doors – and stopped short.

The Central Hall was in chaos.

The entire Museum staff was scurrying about, arguing and waving their hands in the air. Slightly thought she had never before seen so many different types of beard and moustache all in one place. There were shaggy beards and pointy beards, mutton chops and goatees and half-way-down-your-tummy beards, and moustaches that curled, drooped or just plain bushed. And they were *all* wagging agitatedly over the theft. Even the sperm whale skeleton (which was without facial hair of any sort) looked shocked and appalled.

Slightly and Granny made their way through the confusion, down the length of the Hall to where the plundered Dragonfish case stood, just at the foot of the Main Stairs.

The scene of the crime!

Mr Sherlock Holmes would have known just what to look for, thought Slightly, feeling inadequate and a bit despairing. She pulled out her notebook and pencil anyway, and wrote down what she saw.

Exhibition case, picked lock, door hanging open.
Pretty carved Chinese box (wouldn't mind one of those
to keep things in!) with silk padding inside – empty.
Clues to mysterious disappearance – none.
Good person to interview – Professor Appleword.

But, she thought, looking about, *how are we to find one professor amongst so many?* The entire Museum's community was milling about like agitated ants whose nest had been stirred up with a stick.

Except for one . . .

Slightly saw that one of the professors was standing quite still at the edge of the chaos, leaning against a cabinet of birds' beaks. He was tall, terribly pale, with bulging staring eyes, and he had a very peculiar expression on his face. It was the sort of expression that clever detectives would immediately observe and wonder about and probably write down in their notebooks, but Slightly didn't even reach for hers. There was something else about the man that had caught her attention and held it, completely and horribly. It was a drip. A drip that hung from the end of his long, thin, white nose. It was mesmerising, that drip. Would it fall? Wouldn't it fall? Did he even know it was there?

'What are you staring at, Slightly?' scolded Granny,

and then she spotted the man too. 'Ah, excellent. Someone who isn't rushing about. We'll ask him.'

She went right up to him.

'Excuse me, sir,' said Granny politely, though Slightly could see that her eyes, too, kept drifting to the drip. 'Could you kindly tell us where we might find Professor Appleword?'

He said nothing, only stared at them.

'Er, excuse . . . ?' Granny started again.

'Excuse? Excuse?!' snarled the man abruptly. He thrust his thin white face horribly close to Granny's (*so* suddenly, and *so* close, that the drip wavered and threatened to fall right on her and Slightly held her breath . . . the drip stayed put!) and he hissed, 'There *is* no excuse for Professor Appleword. No excuse at all! Professor Appleword should not even *exist*!'

'Why ever not?' exclaimed Granny.

'Why not? Why NOT?! Just look around!'

Slightly and Granny looked. Other than the fussing professors — and the absence of the Dragonfish fossil — the Hall was full of fascinating exhibits on the wonders of Nature.

What does he mean? thought Slightly, confused.

'See?' the man insisted.

'No,' said Slightly.

The man scowled.

'Oh, even a child could understand!' he snapped. 'Appleword clutters the place up with twigs and beaks and stuffed animals and *fossils*, and then – and THEN, he gets asked to show them to the Queen! Do you have any idea how long *I've* been waiting for even a tiny shred of proper recognition? Hmmm? Of course you don't. But I'll tell you. I've been waiting FOREVER! But I never get a chance and it's all *Appleword's* doing. If I had my way I'd fill the Museum with specimens in jars. Hundreds and hundreds of jars! Like this!'

And right then and there, to Slightly's horror, the man pulled a specimen jar out of his pocket. Floating in the peaty liquid was a tiny kangaroo, bleached a pathetic white and holding its little front paws together, its eyes tight shut as if afraid to discover where it was. It was the saddest thing she had ever seen.

'Oh!' whimpered Slightly, thinking of the beautiful terracotta kangaroo at the entrance that she loved so well.

Granny put a comforting hand on her shoulder.

'I think perhaps people don't *want* to just look at specimens in jars,' she said. 'I think they want to look –'

'People?' the man interrupted. 'Who cares about

people?! *I* want to look at specimens in jars! Rooms and rooms of them. Shelf after shelf. And here, in the Central Hall, an *enormous* tank with an entire pickled whale inside – not boring bones but the whole beast! Now *that* would be worth showing to the Queen!' He dropped his voice to a hoarse whisper. 'They don't listen to me, you know. They forget all about me. They even forgot my building till the last minute – that'll have been Appleword's doing, too, I've no doubt! But I'll show him! Oh yes, you just wait . . . an entire whale!' He waved his hands in the air then, abruptly, he and his drip stalked off.

'What an extraordinary man,' murmured Granny Tonic. 'Ah – *there's* Albert!'

Who's Albert? wondered Slightly, still thinking about the sad little kangaroo.

'Lily!'

Slightly stared, even though she knew perfectly well that it wasn't polite, at the harassed-looking man who came rushing up. She wasn't staring because he was so round and short (though he was – extremely round and short). Or because he had no beard at all and a completely bald head, currently turning the colour of a beetroot (though he certainly did). She was staring because he had called Granny Tonic 'Lily'!

I've never heard anybody call her that before, she thought to herself. Several of the Museum staff turned around to stare as well, and Granny Tonic went a tiny bit pink.

'Oh, Lily!' the man repeated and took both her hands in his.

'Professor Appleword,' said Granny in an odd voice, taking her two hands back again.

Hello! thought Slightly, looking at Granny in surprise. *What's all this then?*

But then she remembered why they were here and turned her attention back to the Professor.

Though he was obviously delighted to see Granny, his face immediately crumpled again.

'You find us in a terrible state,' he babbled. 'Terrible. It couldn't be worse. A rare, unique, irreplaceable fossil has been stolen –'

'We know,' said Granny, but he didn't seem to hear.

'– which could not have happened at a worse time – well, it's hard to imagine a *good* time, isn't it? – but when I tell you we are only a week away from a very special Private Viewing –' and here he lowered his voice so that they both needed to lean in close '– and when I say *special*, well, I mean very special *indeed*. It couldn't really be any *more* special.'

'The Queen's Private Viewing. Yes, we heard

people in the crowd outside talking about it,' said Granny.

Professor Appleword's jaw dropped. 'I will never understand how on earth these things get out!' he spluttered. 'Well, it hardly matters now. You must realise what a visit like this means to me – would have meant to me. A Private Viewing by Her Majesty is the highest honour a scientist could hope for! Royal recognition for my fossils, my work – and now . . .'

'Can't you show the Queen your other fossils?' asked Slightly. 'Why is the stolen one so special?'

The Professor peered at her anxiously, as if noticing her for the first time. 'I'm sorry, my dear, I'm particularly frazzled today. Who exactly are you?'

Slightly bobbed a curtsey.

'I'm Slightly Jones,' she said. 'I'm here with, um, Miss Tonic. Very pleased to meet you. And I'd really like to know why the missing fossil is so important.'

The Professor's eyes got all glittery and excited. 'Ah! My Dragonfish is special for two reasons, my dear,' he began. 'Well, I say *my* Dragonfish, though of course it's really the Museum's Dragonfish and before that it was the Mogol of Inner Mongolia's Dragonfish – you remember, Lily, that I travelled there in my younger years? I'm pleased to say the Mogol and I are still friends – I send him Bovril and cricket balls every Christmas, and he sends me the fossils his farmers find when ploughing their fields – charming fellow, really top notch . . . but what was I saying?' He looked confused for a moment, then snapped his fingers. 'Yes, of course. Two reasons. Well, the first is that this fossil may just be the very most exciting thing since Mr Darwin's wonderful book! No doubt you've seen our archaeopteryx? A missing link between lizards and birds? The Dragonfish could very well be just such a missing link, this time between dragons and fish – between myth and science! Oh, if only I could show it to you – the delicate bones of its fins AND the clearest imprint of wings you could possibly wish for – it really is the most beautiful fossil in the entire Museum. And because it's so wonderful, I named it *Dracopisciformia albertii* – and that's the second reason why the Dragonfish is so important!'

'Because you named it after yourself?' asked Granny, looking puzzled.

Slightly also thought this was a little odd, but the Professor was shaking his head.

'No! Well, yes, that's my name too – but I *really* named it after the late Prince Albert.'

Now Slightly understood. Queen Victoria's husband, Prince Albert, had died years ago, but the Queen had never stopped mourning him. She always wore black and she'd had the Albert Memorial and the Albert Hall built in his memory.

'She would have loved *Dracopisciformia albertii,*' murmured Professor Appleword. 'But now . . .'

Slightly's head was humming with questions about the amazing Dragonfish, and the Mogol of Mongolia, and how on *earth* he and the little round person standing before her ever became friends, and could it possibly be that he and *Granny* had once been sweet on each other? Before she could ask anything, though, one of the Museum staff bustled up, drew Professor Appleword aside and whispered in his ear.

'They've arrested him?' the Professor exclaimed.

'He's talking about Mr Thurgood – *finally!*' muttered Granny.

'And the fossil? Did he have it in his possession?' the Professor asked the man.

'Of course he didn't,' muttered Granny. 'Don't be stupid. How could he have it if he never stole it?'

Slightly took one look at Granny's face and thought, *Oh-oh! Watch out!*

And she was right.

Suddenly, it seemed that Granny had had enough!

'ALBERT!' she trumpeted. The sound echoed through the great Hall. Slightly thought Granny might even have stamped her foot as well, but she wasn't sure.

There was a sudden shocked silence in the Hall, and then everyone bustled about again, pretending they hadn't heard. The messenger scurried off like a scared rabbit.

'Albert,' repeated Granny, in a quieter voice. 'The man they've arrested? That's what we've come to talk to you about!'

'You know him?' exclaimed the Professor. 'What – was that who . . . is that the man I hired because you told me to? But Lily, he's your lodger!'

'That's right. Mr Thurgood. We're here to tell you – he has been falsely accused.'

The professor looked distinctly uncomfortable at this.

'Well, but, my dear Lily – as far as I understand it, he *was* alone in the Museum and there were no signs of anyone else having broken in, not anywhere – the police have searched most thoroughly – and all the evidence does *seem* to point to him . . .'

'Mr Thurgood has been falsely accused,' repeated Granny, a little louder this time. She looked at Professor Appleword for a long moment, and then he nodded.

'Then that must be that,' he said quietly. 'Which

means there is the real thief to be found, as well as my Dragonfish. What should I do?'

'Do nothing,' cried Slightly. 'We'll take the case!'

Granny gave her a long hard look. 'What Slightly means,' she said finally, 'is that there is nothing *at this moment* that you should be doing. Even now that you understand the true situation, we realise your word alone still won't free Mr Thurgood. But we will let you know as soon as we find anything –'

'Like clues,' explained Slightly.

'– anything that will lead to the discovery of your stolen fossil and the clearing of our friend's name.' Granny patted the Professor's arm. 'And now we must be going.'

'Please, let me escort you to the door,' said the Professor, as if reluctant to let them go.

Or maybe, thought Slightly, *maybe he's just reluctant to let Granny go!* Then she gave herself a shake. *Focus, Slightly, focus!*

But it was hard to keep her mind on one thing at a time. As they threaded their way through the agitated scientists, Slightly found herself asking a question that was still troubling her. She knew it didn't have anything to do with the case in hand, but she wanted to know the answer.

'Professor Appleword, could I ask . . . when we

came in at first, there was a very peculiar man who seemed really angry at you . . . tall, thin, pale, with a rather, er, wet nose? Who is he and why does he hate you so much?'

'Oh, that would be Professor Octavian Snit,' said Professor Appleword. 'I hope he didn't upset you? He can be . . . difficult. You're right – he has no liking for me or my fossils. He blames me for the way his career has gone. You don't usually see him over here. He usually just lurks about in his own building. Sniffy Snit's Spirit House, we call it.'

'I beg your pardon?' said Granny. 'He is not part of the Museum staff?'

'Oh yes . . . just not part of this *building*. It's tucked in round the back, off Exhibition Road. I . . .' and Professor Appleword lowered his voice as if he didn't want anyone to overhear. 'I don't think he's ever really forgiven us. Well, *me*, really. It was all terribly embarrassing. You see, when we were designing the new museum it was my job to make sure that we planned really, really carefully for just about everything.'

'*Just about* everything?' said Slightly curiously.

'Yes. Just about. We, well, we didn't exactly plan for the wet specimens. Professor Snit's Department. In short, we forgot about them altogether.' At that moment, Slightly thought Professor Appleword looked just like a dog who's done something unmentionable on the carpet.

'What did you do?!' she asked.

'Well, we built him his own building – the Spirit Building – where he could keep all his specimens. It's better that way, being separate from the other collections I mean . . .'

The Spirit Building. Slightly's head immediately filled with pictures of filmy white ghosts in jars, swirling gently up against the glass. There would probably also be low moaning to be heard, and the scent of exotic incense, and . . . At this point she caught up with the conversation again, just as Professor Appleword was saying, '. . . because of the fire risk.'

Slightly was confused. 'I don't understand – I thought you said they were wet? So how can they be a fire risk?' she blurted.

'Ah, well, wet specimens are those stored in alcohol – methylated spirits, in fact – which is very, *very* flammable!'

'And *that's* why it's called the Spirit Building!' Slightly exclaimed.

'Yes. Did you think it was full of ghosts?' The Professor smiled at her.

'No, of course not,' said Slightly firmly, even though that was exactly what she had been thinking.

But there was no time left for more questions.

'Good-bye, Albert,' said Granny.

'Good-bye, Lily,' said Professor Appleword. 'And good-bye, um, Slightly.'

'Good-bye, Professor, and please don't worry!' said Slightly but when she looked back over her shoulder, the little round scientist was still standing there, watching them go, a picture of dejection.

I'll need to re-name the case, she thought. '*The Mystery of the Sad Professor.*'

Chapter Five:
Dank Stone and Misery

The young guard let Slightly and Granny back out with a respectful tug at his hat. As he watched them push their way through the crowd he noticed a small boy scuttling along after them.

What if the boy was a pickpocket – perhaps he should warn the ladies? And then he remembered just how formidable the white-haired one was and decided she could look after herself.

In his opinion, that lady would probably have any foolish pickpocket for breakfast!

Now we have two people to save, Slightly was thinking as they worked their way back through the crowd. *Mr Thurgood and Professor Appleword. Two people to save, a precious fossil to find, and not one clue to be going on with.*

'Well, Slightly, what would your Mr Sherlock Holmes do now?' said Granny. She sounded a bit weary.

Slightly took Granny's arm. 'He'd rush off across town and interview poor Mr Thurgood to within an inch of his life!' she said. 'And Dr Watson would have a notebook full of clues before the day was out!'

But when it came to rushing, London's crowded streets were having none of it. Much precious time was lost as their omnibus inched its way between the carts and cabs, stopping for more passengers than it could very well hold, and causing much bad temper and stepped-on toes. At last, however, they alighted (with difficulty) at the Police Station.

Inside, Slightly recognised the policeman at the desk. He was one of the ones from that morning.

'We are looking for Mr Earnest Thurgood,' said Granny.

'You his landlady?' the policeman said. 'Behind in his rent, is he? Well, you won't find him here.

They've transferred him already … to Newgate Prison.'

'Oh, no!' gasped Slightly. She knew that no prison in all London had a more evil reputation than Newgate. Even Granny paled.

'He's gone, all right,' the policeman continued, sounding quite pleased with himself. 'And there's no point you going on over there now, either. They won't be admitting any more visitors by the time you get there.'

'Not even –' began Slightly, but he waved them away.

'No! Now if you'd like to show yourselves out, I have work to do!' And he stood up and left the room.

Slightly was very satisfied to notice he was walking with a limp.

There was nothing for it but to go home again.

'Don't worry,' said Granny. 'We'll go to Newgate first thing tomorrow morning, and we won't leave until they've let us in to see him.'

They didn't notice the scruffy boy who was still following them – indeed, they had no reason to suspect anyone *of* following them. He tailed them right up to their front door and then melted away into the shadows with a whistle and a grin.

During supper everyone was very subdued. Miss Forth kept welling up and then pretending she wasn't. Mr Westerly's moustache was droopier than Slightly had ever seen it, and Mr Gentler barely ate anything at all. Even the cat was unhappy and kept nosing about everywhere as if looking for something she'd lost.

'Now that's enough borrowing trouble!' said Granny finally, looking around the table. '*Quite* enough. The place may very well not be as bad as we've heard. And just think how useful this experience will be to Mr Thurgood in his writing – why, most novelists would be jealous of him for this opportunity!'

Everyone tried to smile.

Granny is always right, Slightly told herself as she went wearily up to bed. *Detectives never borrow trouble.*

Even so, her pillow was wet by the time she finally fell asleep.

❦

Oh, poor Mr Thurgood! moaned Slightly.

She and Granny were standing outside the forbidding granite front of Newgate. A prison had stood on this site for hundreds of years, and it felt as if the sorrow and suffering of untold thousands had seeped into the grimy stone.

Blacker than Newgate's knocker. Slightly knew

she would never hear that saying again without feeling something of the horror that threatened to overpower her now.

'Chin up and best foot forward, Slightly,' said Granny. It must have been Slightly's imagination that made her think Granny's voice trembled a little. *Nothing* frightened Granny.

They stepped through the door and into a warders' office. A turnkey peered down at them from behind a tall desk.

'Well?' he said. He seemed utterly bored.

'We are here to visit Mr Ernest Thurgood, a recently transferred prisoner!' said Granny. Slightly was relieved to notice that she sounded confident and in control again.

'You his wife?' the turnkey grunted at Granny.

'I am unmarried,' said Granny proudly.

'You his mother?' the turnkey asked, yawning rudely.

'Certainly not!' Granny snapped.

'Well then, you can't see him. It's family only, see, can visit a prisoner and you ain't his family, so you can't.'

Before Granny could say anything to this, Slightly jumped in.

'What about his daughter?' she squeaked.

'Eh?' The man frowned.

'What?' said Granny, but Slightly hurried on.

'You said family can visit. I'm Mr Thurgood's daughter – I'm his family. His only family. Take me to see him, please. My, um, kind and elderly neighbour, Miss Tonic, will wait for me outside, won't you, Miss Tonic?' And Slightly gave Granny a pleading look.

'Oh. Ah. Of course,' coughed Granny. As Slightly passed, however, she heard her mutter, 'Kind and elderly neighbour, indeed!'

The turnkey shrugged and rang a handbell. When another warder appeared he handed Slightly over to him with a curt order to take her to Prisoner Thurgood.

'FOLLOW ME, LITTLE GIRL!' shouted the new man. Slightly winced.

I want to stay with Granny! she whimpered inside her head, but it was too late for that now.

He led her into the heart of the prison, unlocking and then re-locking door after door, each one booming like the lid of a coffin slamming shut. Slightly didn't know what horrors to expect – she didn't want to see *anything*, so she kept her head down and her eyes on the floor. She noticed that the flagstones dipped in the centre, and she couldn't help but think of all the unhappy feet it must have taken to wear down hard stone.

'THIS WAY!' bellowed the turnkey. 'WE'LL GO THROUGH THE EXERCISE YARD!'

Another door to unlock and lock again . . . Slightly looked up. To her surprise, the sky was still there, but the walls of the jail rose so high on every side that most of the yard was in shadow. The walls were pierced with hundreds of small barred windows.

They trudged across the courtyard to another locked door . . .

It's so huge, thought Slightly. *You could be lost for ever in a place so huge.*

Beyond the next door, Slightly found herself in a great long gallery that stretched away before her. It was three storeys high with metal walkways and every few feet there was the shut door of a cell. In spite of a nightmarish silence, she knew that every cell was occupied. Unhappiness, guilt, hopelessness pressed in on her through the stone walls and the thick metal-bound doors. She started to walk forward automatically, but the turnkey was already rattling his key in the lock of one of the nearest doors and called her back.

'YOUR FATHER'S IN HERE! FIVE MINUTES!'

Slightly stumbled forward and the door was slammed to behind her.

'Slightly?! Slightly!'

'Oh!' wailed Slightly, and threw herself into Mr Thurgood's arms. The cell was cold and dark and bare and *awful*, but she was so glad to see him.

'There, now, sit down, my dear. Though there's only the stool, I'm afraid. I can't say how wonderfully glad I am to see you! Did the noisy fellow think I was your father? That was clever of you – I don't think they let anyone but family visit.'

'That – that's right.' Slightly quavered. *Chin forward. Best foot up*, she told herself fiercely. *I'm not going to cry, I'm not going to cry.*

'The air's shocking bad, my dear – I'm not surprised it's making your eyes uncomfortable,' said Mr Thurgood. 'Here, take my hanky.' And he pulled his handkerchief out of his coat pocket and passed it over.

'Oh – you're right,' sniffed Slightly as she took it from him with a weak smile. 'It's the air, I . . . but . . . what's this?'

There was something tucked inside Mr Thurgood's handkerchief!

'It's a folded-up bit of paper. With writing on. Is it yours?'

Mr Thurgood shook his head. 'No. What can it be? How did it get in my pocket? Read it for me, will you, dear? This dim light's too much for me.'

Slightly sniffed hard again, rubbed her sleeve across her eyes (in a way that Granny Tonic would not have approved), unfolded the paper, and peered at it.

'It is hard to read, but it looks like . . . it is! It's a riddle!' She read aloud,

> *We are not only bodies*
> *This we all know*
> *In the house of bodies' final rest*
> *I rest below.'*

Slightly and Mr Thurgood stared at each other.

'Well,' said Mr Thurgood. 'I've heard better!'

'Me too, but more importantly, what does it mean?' cried Slightly, and her detective's heart began to jump about in her chest.

'I wonder how it got into my handkerchief?' continued Mr Thurgood.

'Me too – but *what does it mean*?' repeated Slightly – before either could answer there was a horrible clanging and rattling at the cell door.

'TIME'S UP!' bellowed the turnkey.

'There's really no need to shout,' said Mr Thurgood mildly. 'We're right here.'

'I LIKE TO SHOUT,' shouted the turnkey. 'AND YOU'RE IN NO POSITION TO TELL ME NOT TO!'

Mr Thurgood sighed. The noisy man was right about that.

'I'll take the paper with me – it's a Clue!' whispered Slightly, as she gave Mr Thurgood a daughterly kiss on the cheek. 'Goodbye, dear father,' she added in a louder voice, and she followed the turnkey out of the cell. As he slammed the metal door shut with a great clang, she caught a last glimpse of Mr Thurgood. He was trying hard to look brave, but he *really* looked so small and forlorn, locked up and all alone in that awful place, that Slightly couldn't help herself.

She started to sob, much to the turnkey's embarrassment.

'CHEER UP, MISS! IF YOU LIKE, I COULD TAKE YOU TO SEE WHERE WE BURY THE MURDERERS UNDER THE FLAGSTONES – WE CALL IT DEAD MAN'S WALK,' he offered. 'YOU CAN SEE THE INITIALS SCRATCHED ON THE WALL AND EVERYTHING!'

He seemed surprised when this only made Slightly cry even harder.

'Or I could try to not shout,' he said reluctantly. 'If you thought that would help.'

Slightly sniffed, then smiled wetly. 'That's very . . . nice of you,' she said. 'Thank you. It would help a lot.'

'RIGHT!' he shouted, and then stopped. 'Right,' he said in what he probably thought was a whisper. 'I'll try.'

CHAPTER SIX:
Cryptic Clue

As Slightly stepped out of the prison, the sunshine felt too bright. Granny took one look at her, immediately tucked her under her wing and whisked her away at a brisk pace. She wouldn't let Slightly speak until they had each swallowed a hot mug of coffee from a coffee stall. Then she stopped a passing Muffin Man and bought two of his finest. Nearby there was a grimy little city park and Granny settled them both on a blackened bench.

'There,' she said. 'Eat first and then you can tell me everything.'

Slightly did as she was told. (It was surprising how comforting a muffin could be.) Then she told Granny as much as she could bear of the horrors of Newgate. And *then* she showed Granny what she and Mr Thurgood had found in his pocket.

Granny stared thoughtfully at the writing.

'It's a riddle,' she said slowly. 'Someone put a riddle in Mr Thurgood's pocket. I suppose the questions we need to ask are who, when and why. I suggest you make use of your notebook . . .'

She's right, thought Slightly. *Detectives are methodical, even when they're upset.* She wrote down the left-hand side of a page: *Who? When? Why?*

Slightly looked at the three words and pulled on one of her ears to try to make her mind work better.

'Right,' she said. 'When. When could someone have put a riddle in Mr Thurgood's pocket? In prison? Or in the Police Station? Or during his arrest?'

'Not easily,' said Granny, shaking her head. 'Unless it was a policeman, but that doesn't seem likely.'

'No . . . Which means it must have been put in his pocket *before* all that. Sometime on his way to work on Sunday night or on the way home on Monday morning. Don't you think?'

'I do. Which leaves the question of who, and why?' said Granny.

'I don't know about who, but *why* do you give anybody a riddle?' said Slightly, sitting up straighter. 'Because you want them to figure out the answer, is why! Somebody *wanted* the answer to this riddle to be known, Granny, I'm sure of it. And what is the one thing that Mr Thurgood – and Professor Appleword – desperately need to know right now?'

'Where the Dragonfish is?'

'Yes!' cried Slightly. 'I'm almost absolutely certain that this riddle is telling us exactly where it is! And all we have to do is . . .'

'Solve it?'

'Yes!'

'All right. Carry on,' said Granny calmly.

Slightly slumped again. Solve it! Just like that! She wished she could take her brain out of her head and give it a good shake. *Think, Slightly, think!* But it was too hard. She was tired and upset and not in the mood for riddles and games. *But this isn't a game*, she scolded herself. *This is deadly serious!*

She pulled out her notebook and pencil and wrote carefully:

We are not only bodies
This we all know
In the house of bodies' final rest
I rest below.

'Just look at it one bit at a time,' said Granny sensibly. 'Remember, no butterfly ever became Prime Minister. Start with *We are not only bodies . . .*'

Slightly put down the notebook and pencil, took hold of her ears and pulled hard. She thought, *We are not only bodies . . . What's not a body . . . a head? . . . what's a house of rest . . . a bedroom? a bed? . . . but it's below, so . . . the Dragonfish head is under a bed? No, no, no, that makes no sense – stop being so stupid!*

And then, very slowly, Slightly's brain began to work.

'Granny,' she said, letting go of her ears and picking up her pencil again.

'Yes, dear,' said Granny.

'*We are not only bodies.*'

'Yes, dear?'

'What if . . . *not bodies* . . . means souls?'

'Yes . . .'

'And *the house of bodies' final rest* . . . could that be . . . a coffin?' said Slightly.

'Then the answer to the riddle would be 'Souls' Coffin' . . . I don't think that sounds right. And it's *below*. What's below a coffin?'

'More coffins? Dirt? No, that's no good.' Slightly slumped.

'Well, what else can be a resting place?'

'House . . . resting place . . . *final* resting place . . .'

Just then, bells began to sound the hour. First one church and then another expressed its opinion of what the exact time was, until, at last, St Paul's rang out. *Mine*, it seemed to say, *mine is the last word*. Granny and Slightly turned and looked at each other, delight blossoming on their faces.

'House of bodies' final resting place –'

'– is a church – and under a church is –'

'– a crypt!'

'But which crypt – lots of churches have –'

'Wait, no, it's all there – *This we all know* – ALL – *not bodies* – SOULS – *house of final rest* – CHURCH – *below* – CRYPT!'

'It's in the crypt of All Souls' Church!' they chorused, far too loudly for a public place.

'There's an All Souls' Church at Langham Place,' said Granny, standing up and straightening her hat vigorously.

'What are we waiting for?' cried Slightly. 'Look – there's an omnibus coming now!'

But Granny was having none of that.

'Omnibus?' she said. 'I think not. For this, we're taking a cab!' And she waved her umbrella at a passing hansom.

The cabman pulled back on his horse's reins and

peered down at them from his high perch.

'Where to, ladies?' he said.

'All Souls' Church in Langham Place,' said Granny. 'Do you know it?'

The cabman laughed. 'What – the ugliest church in all of London? Of course I know it. Though why you'd want to go there when you're practically on the doorstep of the most beautiful, St Paul's, I *don't* know.' He looked at her expectantly.

'That's a long story,' said Granny, and then, without saying another word, she climbed into the cab.

Slightly laughed at the disappointment on the man's face and clambered in after Granny.

Unnoticed, a scruffy boy with a determined expression on his face came running after them as they set off. In mid-stride he leapt at the back of the cab and clung there, grinning, inches from the cobbles, between the spinning wheels, an extra passenger that no one knew about . . .

'Well, when it came down to it, it wasn't a hard riddle at all!' said Slightly smugly. She knew she was sounding boastful but she couldn't help it. She'd done it! She'd solved the mystery! She'd solved the case and saved the day! Not all heroines had to be beautiful and blonde and tall; sometimes they were ginger-haired and ferrety!

'So it would seem,' said Granny but strangely, there seemed to be some doubt in her voice now.

'Mr Thurgood is going to be so happy. And –' here Slightly gave Granny a sideways look, 'Professor Appleword – he'll be happy too, won't he, Granny?'

'Yes . . . he will.' Did Slightly see an odd expression come across Granny's face? Or did she just imagine it?

'He seems very nice,' Slightly added, fishing gently. But Granny's mind was elsewhere.

'We still have no answer to the question of *who?*' she murmured. 'What kind of person steals something, hides it, and then makes sure the owner can find it again?'

'A crazy person! Who cares – we're going to find the Dragonfish!'

'A crazy person . . . or a sane person with a plan . . .'

But Slightly wasn't going to listen. *I am not at home to doubts*, she thought firmly. Instead, she shut her eyes and wished that the hansom cab horse was a stolen racer. She imagined them careening through the streets, scattering pedestrians, spooking all the other vehicles, overturning the carts of the vendors and crossing the city like a flood in a sewer . . .

When she opened her eyes, however, it was

obvious that their horse was no thoroughbred and none of the other users of the road were in any danger from his turn of speed.

Detectives have to be patient, Slightly told herself. So she spent the rest of the journey feeling pleased with herself, excited about what would come next and mildly curious to know just how ugly All Souls' Church really was, since she'd never seen it before.

At last, as they pulled into Regent Street, the cabman called down, 'There it is. Much good may it do you!'

'Oh!' said Slightly.

All Souls' wasn't so much ugly as . . . *surprising*. It faced into the street at an angle, with a curving set of steps leading to a round porch of columns, another, much smaller circle of columns above and a strange very pointy tower to top the lot. At first glance, Slightly felt she quite liked it, but the cabman's opinion hadn't changed.

'What an eyesore,' he muttered as he took the fare from Granny. 'Shouldn't ought to be allowed.' And with that he drove away.

'Who will let us into the crypt?' Slightly asked Granny, but as luck would have it, the answer to her question was at that moment sweeping the front steps.

'I expect that is the sexton,' said Granny. 'We will ask him.'

The sexton was an old man. As they came up closer to him, Slightly became aware of a musty, unpleasant smell wafting off him with each sweep of the broom. She couldn't help noticing that his hands were oddly stained and his fingernails were long, yellow and cracked – and when he smirked at them she saw that his teeth were the same.

'Ma'am and Miss,' the man smarmed, twisting his body in a peculiarly horrible way that was more of a grovel than a bow. 'Miss and Ma'am. Can I be of assistance?'

'Yes, Mr, er . . .?' said Granny.

'I'm Morbley, Ma'am.'

'Mr Morbley, I was wondering –'

'Nay. Just Morbley,' he said, showing more of his horrible teeth. 'Sexton of All Souls'. Been planting 'em, rich and poor, these fifty years and always been just plain Morbley. Ah, fifty years, Ma'am and Miss, boy and man, I've dug and delved. Buried 'em all. Boy and man.'

Unbidden, a picture of a boy Morbley came into Slightly's mind, all yellowed and twisted and smelly, but with a child's face. She pushed the thought away with a shudder.

Meanwhile, Granny was saying, 'As sexton, would you be the person to speak to about visiting the crypt? We'd very much like to see it, if you'd be so kind?'

'Aye, Morbley's your man.' With another spasm, he pulled a ring of keys out of his coat pocket. 'Funny you should say that, though. Powerful lot of interest in our old crypt there's been these days,' he said as, very slowly, one at a time, he held each of the keys up to his old eyes and peered at it for an agonisingly long time, before rejecting it and starting all over again.

Slightly was beginning to think she would be as old as Morbley himself by the time he identified the right key, but at last he found the one he wanted.

'Aye, powerful lot . . . this way, ladies.' And he led them into the lobby of the church. To one side, they could see an ornate grill in the floor. Grunting and wheezing, Morbley knelt down and inserted the key in the lock. As Slightly and Granny watched, he pulled back the grill like a trap door and let it clang on the stone flags. Then, with excruciating care, he lit a lantern for himself and a candle for each of them, before leading them down a flight of stone stairs, down into a damp, dark, low-roofed space.

The crypt.

'Mind your steps, Ma'am and Miss, mind your steps,' he warned, and his voice echoed strangely in the enclosed space. The smell Slightly had noticed coming from their guide was much more intense here. It was a wet smell, made up of odours of disturbed earth and other things it wasn't good to think about too closely.

'It's not as if we've anybody famous down here,' Morbley muttered on. 'A duke or two at most, but I think you'll find they moulder away just like an ordinary gentleman. Sarcophagus or shroud – not a lot of difference once the damp gets in . . . unless you're a tanner by trade. They last, do tanners, more years than you'd think likely. But not ordinary folk. Not like you and me.'

He let his lantern swing back and forth on his finger, and stared at them as if judging just how long *they* would keep out the damp. Granny was looking distinctly uncomfortable, but Slightly had had enough.

She held her candle high and started to search about by its flickering light.

It must be here, she thought. *It must!*

Into corners and behind stacked tools . . . in the shadow of stone coffins and a pile of split wooden caskets, stacked precariously up to the ceiling . . .

disturbing a nest of something that squeaked and fled in all directions . . .

Detectives don't scream, Slightly told herself, panting a little. *Mr Holmes never screamed.*

And then – she found it. It wasn't even very well hidden. It was just lying there, next to some sacks of quicklime, by the end wall. It shone in the dim flicker of the candlelight, white and clean and strangely innocent.

'Granny!' she screamed.

'Oh now, has the little girl hurt herself?' grumbled Morbley. 'It's not a playground down here, you know. I'll not take any blame if she's hurt herself.'

'No, no, Mr, I mean, Morbley. I don't think she's injured. I think she's found something. If we could just bring the light closer . . .'

Granny seemed to have forgotten her earlier doubts. Now she practically grabbed the lantern out of the old man's hands and rushed over to where Slightly was standing – and together they looked down at the object of their search, there on the uneven floor.

The Dragonfish lay on its side, slightly curled, as if it had only just fallen asleep. It had a small head with a pointed snout like a fox. A delicate tracery of bones showed its ribs and fins – and there, laid back along its spine, the impression of a pair of wings was plain to see.

'It's beautiful, isn't it,' Slightly murmured, and Granny nodded.

'Oh, that,' said the old gravedigger as he peered over their shoulders. 'There was a man put that there not so long ago. Can't remember who he said he was. Maybe he didn't say. But I *do* remember him saying how somebody'd be coming for it sometime soon and they'd give me a penny and take it away.' And he put out a stained, taloned hand.

'What? Oh. Yes, of course,' said Granny, and she rummaged in her purse and gave the old man his penny. 'Now, what can you tell us about the man who brought this here?'

But the moment the coin was in his hand, Morbley's brain seemed to stop functioning.

'Man? What man?' he mumbled. 'Don't know nothing about no man. If you ladies has seen enough, I've work to do.' And he headed for the crypt stairs, taking the lantern with him.

Granny and Slightly had no choice.

'Wait, Mr Morbley!' called out Granny. 'We're coming too!'

And then she and Slightly carried the Dragonfish up into the daylight.

CHAPTER SEVEN:
Smashing Success

The gravedigger showed them out of the church and then promptly disappeared.

'I would have liked to ask him a good deal more,' muttered Granny, but Slightly was feeling too happy to care about mouldy old men.

She was singing under her breath, 'We found it! We found it!' and looking forward to seeing Professor Appleword's face!

At the top of the church steps, however, they paused. How were they to get their wonderful find from All Souls' Church all the way to the

Museum? It was too bulky to take on a crowded omnibus and Granny didn't have enough money left in her purse for another hansom cab.

'We'll send a note to Professor Appleword,' she decided. 'I know he'll be happy to send the Museum cart and horse over for us – especially when he hears what we have with us!'

Slightly agreed this was an excellent idea.

There would be no problem finding a messenger. There were always street children about, thin and sharp-faced, perpetually on the lookout for an errand to run or a horse to hold. Anything for the chance of a coin to spend on something hot from a vendor or a bed for the night.

Slightly gave Granny a page from her notebook and her propelling pencil to write with. As she finished the note, Granny looked about and, indeed, there was a dirty-looking lad with brown eyes watching them from the foot of the curved church steps.

'I'll send it with him,' she said, but Slightly wasn't really paying attention. She couldn't stop looking at the Dragonfish, like a new mother with her baby.

'That was odd,' said Granny as she returned. 'When I asked him if he knew where the Natural History Museum was, he seemed to think the question was very funny.'

Slightly looked up. 'Really? I wonder why?' she said. She caught a brief glimpse of the boy disappearing amongst the crowds in the street, and frowned. She felt as if there was something about him that she should have noticed, though she wasn't sure what. It made her uneasy for a moment, then she forgot.

You're beautiful, she told the Dragonfish fossil. *And I found you!*

The street boy may have been unsettling, but he was also fast! Sooner than either Granny or Slightly would have thought possible, a horse-drawn cart trundled up to the church.

The young guard they'd met the day before jumped down and ran up the steps to them.

'Is it true?' he panted. 'Did you really find it?'

Slightly had wrapped the Dragonfish in a bit of spare sacking from the crypt. Now she lifted an edge of the rough cloth and proudly showed him.

The young guard whistled appreciatively.

'We'd better be getting this back, then,' he said with a grin. 'Don't you think?'

He helped Granny up onto the seat, settled Slightly in the bed of the cart, and handed her the Dragonfish.

'Was Professor Appleword pleased to get our note?'

she called to him as he encouraged the Museum horse to its best pace.

'I'll say!' he replied. 'He let out such a yell, I'd be surprised if it wasn't heard from one end of the building to the other!'

As it turned out, the young guard was absolutely right about that. Carrying the wrapped-up Dragonfish, he led Granny and Slightly up the steps of the Natural History Museum, through the big front doors and into a Central Hall *full* of excited staff! But unlike the day before, now the moustaches and mutton chops and beards were all waggling with joy.

Professor Appleword was standing at the far end of the Hall, at the foot of the main stairs, a look of I-hardly-dare-believe-it all over his shiny face.

With a bow, the guard held out the bundled fossil.

'I think this honour should be yours, ladies,' he said gallantly.

Let me! Let me! Let me! begged Slightly silently. She didn't say anything out loud, but it was clearly written all over her face as she looked at Granny . . .

Granny smiled. 'All right, dear,' she said. 'If you're sure you can manage.' She carefully unwrapped the sacking covering the Dragonfish, and the young guard handed the precious burden to Slightly.

As she began to walk forward, she heard whispers of excitement on every side.

'Is it true?'

'Is that it?'

'I do believe she's got it!'

Slightly could feel the grin on her face getting bigger by the second.

I did it, she thought. *I solved the case! I saved the day!*

She knew it was wrong to boast, even inside her own head, but at that moment she didn't care – at that moment she knew she was a heroine!

Mr Thurgood is going to be so grateful, maybe he'll put me in his book! And maybe Professor Appleword might name a fossil after me – how wonderful that would be! And Queen Victoria – she'll get to see the Dragonfish now, and she'll be so grateful, that maybe . . .

Maybe if Slightly hadn't been so busy thinking about these things, she might have avoided the disaster that was just about to happen. Maybe she might have noticed the walking stick which was so suddenly shoved into her path, right where her legs were bound to tangle with it . . .

'Watch out!' someone cried, but it was already too late.

There was a sharp pain in her shin – her feet

stopped moving forward but the rest of her carried on – all around her she could see faces, open-mouthed, wide-eyed, frozen in dismay – she was falling, falling, and with her hands full of fossil she couldn't save herself – and then even that started to slip out of her control and –

CRASH!

Slightly landed hard on the stone floor. The priceless, wonderful, utterly unique Dragonfish fossil flew up and out of her hands in a graceful arc, and then *smashed* down. Smashed – and shattered into a thousand pieces.

There was a moment of total, appalled silence. Then Professor Appleword slowly bent down and picked up one of the fragments that had landed near his feet. He looked at it in bewilderment.

'It shouldn't have done that,' he murmured, turning the piece back and forth.

The tears were pricking in Slightly's eyes and she felt as if she were going to be sick. *What have I done?* she wailed to herself. *What have I done?*

'Are you hurt, dear?' a strange professor asked kindly as he helped her up, but she could only shake her head. She couldn't speak.

'It shouldn't have done that,' said Professor Appleword again, louder this time.

'It was an accident,' someone replied. 'The girl didn't *mean* to drop it!'

But the Professor shook his head and held out the fragment with trembling hands.

'No, I mean it shouldn't have done THAT . . .'

Before he could explain any further, there was Professor Octavian Snit, pushing his way through the crowd.

'What terrible thing has happened here?' he cried. He bent to pick up a piece of the debris. 'Oh no! Is this . . . it can't be . . . the Flagondish we've been hearing so much about? Professor Appleword's *jewel*?' And then he squeezed his fist and the piece of fossil crumbled, just like that, between his fingers.

As one, every person in the room gasped in horror.

'But how is this possible?' said Snit. 'Have I suddenly acquired superhuman strength, that I can crush stone?'

Stop! thought Slightly. *Stop!*

She didn't understand what he meant but she *knew* he was making things worse. She tried to speak through her sobs but there was no chance. Professor Snit was grabbing broken bits, waving them under the other professors' noses, and then crumbling them to dust.

'This is unbelievable,' he shouted. 'Just look at

this! This isn't a fossil at all! It's *terracotta*! It's made out of the same material as the decorations all around us. Do you realise what this means, gentlemen? Do you? It means that this so-called fossil – the fossil that Professor Albert Appleword has been bragging about – this unique, *jewel* in our collection – IS A FAKE!'

Protests broke out all over the room, but as more and more of the scientists examined the fragments, their voices died away into a deep, horrified silence.

Which Professor Snit filled with more poisonous words.

'And to think, Her Majesty, Queen Victoria herself, was going to come to view this . . . this . . . *fraud*!' he murmured, but loudly enough that everyone could hear. 'The Natural History Museum was going to show our beloved monarch a lie, passed off as scientific truth by *that man*. Can you imagine the shame? Can you imagine the stain this would have put on the reputation of this museum? *And* I understand he let the night-watchman take the blame – the act of a coward if ever I heard of one! Someone better rush off right away and get the poor man out of Newgate Prison before he has to spend another moment in that terrible place, for he is clearly as innocent as . . . as this little girl!'

Everyone looked at Slightly, who gulped but couldn't stop crying, and then at Professor Appleword. He stood there, white-faced and stricken, as if trapped in some appalling nightmare.

But Professor Snit had no mercy. As one of the Museum staff hurried away to get Mr Thurgood out of prison, he continued relentlessly. 'I can only thank heaven – and this little girl – for clearing the night-watchman's name, and for showing *Appleword* up for what he really is, before it was too late. What he really is – a *cheat*.' Professor Snit turned his face away and shook his head as if in sorrow, but Slightly could see there was a horrible little smile on his lips. Just then, she hated him more than she had ever hated anyone in her entire life.

'It isn't true,' she sobbed angrily. '*You're* the cheat.'

But no one was listening to her. They were all too busy twittering and whispering to each other like a flock of shocked starlings. A circle of empty space formed around Professor Appleword. All backs were half turned away from him and nobody seemed willing to meet his eye. Everyone pretended he wasn't even there.

Except Slightly . . .

. . . and Granny Tonic. One on either side, they led Professor Appleword away. He didn't resist. Pale and lost, he looked as broken as the terracotta pieces on the museum floor. Two words kept coming from his lips, so quietly they could hardly hear what he said.

'A fake,' he whispered. 'A fake . . .'

Chapter Eight:
Disgrace

They took him home.

'He can have my room, Granny,' said Slightly. 'I'll sleep in the kitchen.' She was feeling so guilty and miserable over what had happened that she wished there was something much, much bigger she could give poor Professor Appleword, but this was all she could think of.

'Thank you, dear, that would be best,' agreed Granny. 'He'll need some peace and quiet for now.'

The Professor hardly seemed to know where he was but they helped him to take off his shoes and left him to rest on Slightly's bed.

'At least Mr Thurgood will be able to come home,' said Slightly as they tiptoed downstairs. 'Will it be long, do you think?'

'No,' said Granny. 'I'm sure we'll be seeing him very soon indeed.'

And she was right. When they stepped into the kitchen, there was Mr Thurgood, already released from that horrible cell and drinking tea with Miss Forth, Mr Gentler and Mr Westerly.

'The Museum fellow couldn't have been nicer,' he burbled delightedly. 'He apologised ever so many times, and brought me home in a cab! He said I could absolutely have the night off, but I said no. I'm much too happy to sleep, and it'll be good to be back at work.'

'And I'm making my Red Herring Pies for tea,' said Miss Forth. 'To celebrate!'

'Oh,' said Granny and Slightly. Miss Forth's Red Herring Pies were delicious, but it was hard to feel happy about food after the day they'd had.

'Perhaps that will help Professor Appleword feel better,' added Slightly, though she wasn't really sure that *anything* would do that.

'A Professor? Here? Oh!' And Miss Forth was all

set to start fluttering about having a stranger eat her pie when Mr Gentler interrupted.

'What's wrong?' he asked, looking at Granny and Slightly. 'Something has happened, hasn't it? You must tell us everything.'

Slightly looked at them all and part of her thought, *It seems a shame – they're all so happy.* But the rest of her wanted to tell *everything* – every boastful thought and mistaken glory, every stage of the pride that went before the fall. So that was what she did. By the time the tale was finished, the first batch of Red Herring Pies was ready to come out, but nobody felt hungry any more. Miss Forth set them to cool by the back door and popped the next lot into the oven to bake.

'I take it we don't believe that what you found was your Professor's *original* fossil – he wasn't trying to trick anyone?' said Mr Westerly. Before Granny and Slightly could explode, he raised his hand calmingly. 'That's what I thought. Well, then, it seems to me you did them all a favour by smashing that fake fossil.' And he gave Slightly a comforting pat on the shoulder with his big, paint-stained hand. 'It's best to know what we're dealing with.'

'But what *are* we dealing with?' asked Miss Forth. 'Why would anyone want the fossil to be found, after going to all the trouble of stealing it?'

'That's what Granny said,' muttered Slightly. *And I wouldn't listen*, she added in anguish to herself. *A real detective would have listened!*

'Someone wanted you to find the fake,' said Mr Gentler, tapping the table with a thoughtful rhythm.

'But it *looked* so real! How could they make it look so real?!' wailed Slightly.

'Same way they made all the decorations at the Museum,' Mr Westerly answered. 'Make a mould, pour in the terracotta – or in this case it might be white clay – bake it and there you go. Of course, Mr Waterhouse had to have his things carved first, but the principle's the same.'

Granny started to say something, when Slightly looked up. 'So does that mean . . . does that mean the real Dragonfish could still be out there?' she asked, her voice wobbling a little.

'Oh, yes, most likely. Making a mould from something doesn't harm it,' said Mr Westerly.

'So that means there's still hope!' cried Slightly. Then she slumped down dejectedly again. 'If only we knew where to look. The riddle led us to the horrible fake fossil, but *now* what do we do?'

'There's another answer to the riddle,' said a strange voice. 'I heard the geezer say so, gloating away to hisself. He said, "I'm going to tell them exactly where they *both* are and they'll still be too stupid to find anything but the fake!" So, see, you only guessed one so far.'

Everyone in the kitchen froze. There, just inside the doorway from the garden, and looking as if he might disappear back into it at any second, was a scruffy boy. He had bright brown eyes and mud-coloured hair and . . .

He looks familiar, thought Slightly.

'Who are you?' she demanded.

'None of your business. Who are *you*, for that matter – hey, Missus, you shouldn't let your slavey talk so fresh!' This was directed to Granny, who hid a smile and said,

'Her name is Slightly Jones and she is not my slavey, she is my great-niece.'

The boy sniffed. 'She don't look so great to me,' he grunted. 'Why's she call you *Granny* then?'

'How do you know I call her Granny?' blurted Slightly. Then it hit her. Without realising it, she'd been seeing this ragged boy all day.

'You've been following us!' she exclaimed indignantly.

The boy grinned. 'Oh, you finally noticed that, did you? You took your time!' And he stuck out his tongue at her in a provoking – and familiar! – way.

'Why *have* you been following these ladies, young man,' said Mr Westerly. He didn't mean to sound fierce, but his moustache was bristling alarmingly and the boy edged closer to the door.

'I ain't talking to a roomful,' he said. 'Just you, Missus, and the girl, if I have to.'

'Of course,' said Granny mildly. 'If you wouldn't mind?' she added to the boarders.

'Yes.'

'Oh, of course.'

'Indeed. If you'd just mind the pies?'

Out they trooped and gently shut the door, but Slightly knew for a fact that each and every one would be lingering in the hallway, eavesdropping till their ears flapped. And she didn't blame them one bit. 'When did you start following us?' Granny asked. 'Was it before I paid you to deliver the note for us? That *was* you, wasn't it?'

'Of course it was!' said the boy. 'I've been trailing you for days. Well, two days, anyway.'

'You were outside the Museum,' said Slightly accusingly. 'You stuck your tongue out at me then, too!'

'That's right,' he agreed cheerfully. 'I was just about to give up hanging round since it was clear nobody knew it was me nicked the thing, and there was no sign of the geezer who'd hired me – and then I saw you two, all bustling and purposeful-like. "Hello," I thought, "this looks promising." And didn't you march right in when no one else was allowed? Interesting people, you seemed to me. "There'll be some needful in this," I thought, "and no mistake." Better than the geezer who hired me.'

'The geezer who . . . ?' murmured Granny.

'The man what asked me to steal the fossil from the Museum – oh, and slip the bit of paper into that gentleman's pocket unnoticeable like afterwards. He asked, and I did and then – would you believe it? – he refused to pay me. He said he'd hand me over to the rozzers if he ever saw my face again. He said. And it ain't fair not to pay,' he ended with a whine.

'I'll pay you,' said Granny.

'What?!' exclaimed Slightly.

'How much?' said the boy at the same time. 'And what do you want me to nick?'

'I don't want you to nick anything,' said Granny. 'What I want is information. I will pay for your honest answers. And, as well, you will have the chance to – how shall I put it – save the day?'

'I don't mind.' He shrugged.

No! cried Slightly silently. *I want to save the day! I want it to be me!* Nevertheless, she took out her notebook and prepared to collect clues.

'So now, what we want to know is: exactly who hired you to steal the fossil from the Natural History Museum?' said Granny.

'I don't know,' the boy said. 'We don't ask for names in my line of work.' When Granny raised an eyebrow, he explained, 'You'd just be asking for a lie, Missus.'

'Ah,' said Granny, nodding. 'Quite. Anonymity amongst thieves.'

'Wot?' The boy squinted at her and wiped his nose on his sleeve.

'It means not telling your name,' said Granny as she handed him her hanky.

'Rum fogle – ta!' said the boy, looking at the handkerchief appreciatively. It then disappeared into his pocket quicker than magic, and he proceeded to use his sleeve again.

Slightly waited for Granny to say something, but she just smiled.

Huh, thought Slightly. *She'd never let me get away with that!*

'Do you have a cold?' she said, pointedly. She meant to sound grown-up and distant, but she mostly just sounded rude. Granny gave her a look, but the boy didn't seem to care.

'Not me,' he boasted. 'I never get sick. Tell you what, though, the geezer we're speaking on – I bet *he* had a cold. Leastways he had this big old wet drip hangin' off the end of his nose the whole time. But *he* never wiped it – no manners, him – he just let it hang there. Disgusting, really. Could have landed on *any*body, that drip could have!'

'SNIT!' cried Slightly, jumping up.

'Same to you!' said the boy, edging back towards the open door in alarm.

'She means *Professor* Snit,' said Granny soothingly. 'The scientist from the Museum. That could be the name of the man who hired you. Professor Octavian Snit.'

'Phew – what a moniker!' whistled the boy. 'Though, come to think of it, it suits him!'

'That's definitely a clue, wouldn't you say, Granny?' said Slightly excitedly.

Granny nodded. 'I would indeed. That's worth a penny, right there.' And she pulled out her purse and gave him a penny, which disappeared just as quickly as the hanky.

'Ta, Missus,' said the boy. 'You're more of a gentleman than that Snot!'

'Snit,' said Granny. 'Just out of interest, what were you hoping to charge him for the job?'

The boy ticked the items off on his fingers. 'Well, there was basic rate for the nab, plus public building increment, plus flash area danger money –' he noticed the confusion on their faces and added, 'You know, where it's flash it's harder to find a nice dark dirty alley to scarper down and there's more rozzers about to find *you*.'This explanation seemed to satisfy Granny, though Slightly was still bewildered. 'And then there's your final adjustment up or down depending on the quality of the client's wipe.'

'Wipe . . . Oh, you mean handkerchief!' said Granny. 'I see! You judge how much the, ah, client is able to afford based on how fine or otherwise their handkerchief is. How ingenious!'

'But,' Slightly frowned, 'how do you *know* what their handkerchief's like?'

The boy looked at her as if she were more than a bit dim. 'I nick it, of course,' he said.

Slightly could feel herself beginning to seethe. She drew in breath to tell this pipsqueak just exactly what she thought of him – when Granny's warning voice came.

'Slightly! Think first!'

The boy looked puzzled for a moment and then that irritating grin came back.

'Oh, I get it,' he said. 'Got a temper, eh? That'll

be the carrot top in 'er coming out.'

Slightly glared at him as hard as she could, but he only laughed. *One more word from him and I'll walk right out*, she thought, but she knew she wouldn't. She didn't want to miss anything, no matter *how* annoying the boy was!

'Thank you, young man,' said Granny. 'You have given us a great deal to think about. Will we be able to find you if any more questions come to mind?'

'Don't you worry, Missus. I'll be around! Bye for now!'

'No, wait,' cried Slightly. 'We don't even know your name!'

'I should tell you my name?!' the boy scoffed. 'Not likely!'

'I already know it anyway,' said Slightly, thinking fast. She picked up Mr Westerly's newspaper and pointed at the words, *LONDON FOG*, at the top of the page. 'Isn't that your name, right there?'

The boy took a step forward and squinted at the paper, first with his head on one side, then on the other. Then he skipped back and grinned his irritating grin at her.

'Ain't me,' he said. 'That'll be some other bloke's name.'

'You can't read, can you?' said Slightly.

'I can read well enough to know my name if I see it on a Wanted Poster,' he said with a shrug.

In spite of herself, Slightly was impressed. 'There are Wanted Posters of you?' she asked.

'Course not!' the boy scoffed. 'I'm too good. In fact, I'm *so* good, the rozzers don't even know they want me! But if they ever did, I'd be the first to know, 'cause Matthew Bone I can read as well as you can. Maybe better.'

'So your name is Matthew Bone,' said Slightly.

There was a short, busy pause.

'You tricked me!' said Matthew accusingly.

Slightly shrugged. 'You tricked yourself,' she said. But she felt pretty smug anyway.

'Fair enough. I'm off,' and he moved towards the door again.

'You're just *leaving*?' said Slightly. She was surprised. 'Don't you want to get back at Snit? Don't you want to get justice? Don't you want to find out what happens next?'

'Don't you want to take some pies with you?' said Granny quietly.

Matthew looked back over his shoulder with a cheeky grin all over his dirty face. 'Ah, Missus,' he said. 'You know I already have!'

And with that, he was gone.

The others filed back in, but the room seemed strangely quiet now he'd left.

'Where would Snit find a boy like that?' mused Mr Westerly.

'Thieves' Market,' said Granny. 'Friday's hiring day.'

And, for the hundredth time, Slightly Jones wondered how Granny knew these things. Life was full of unsolved mysteries. But that made her think of poor Professor Appleword upstairs in her bed, and that just made her feel sad.

'Well, we have another clue,' said Granny.

'Or the same clue again, if the riddle is what you mean,' said Mr Thurgood. 'But I can no more solve it this time than I could have the time before. Thank goodness we've got our very own detective Slightly on the case!' And he looked hopefully at her.

But Slightly could only shake her head. She had no new ideas. She had no old ones either. She was too tired to think at all any more.

'We'll let it be for now,' said Granny, getting up with a sigh. 'It's late, and we all need to rest. And who knows? The answer may just come when we least expect it.'

They ate Miss Forth's excellent pies, Mr Thurgood left for the Museum, and the other lodgers headed for bed.

'Goodnight, Granny.'

'Goodnight, Miss Forth. Mr Gentler. Sleep well, Mr Westerly.'

'Goodnight.'

Together Granny and Slightly made up a pallet bed by the range. Granny climbed the stairs to the top of the house and Slightly snuggled in with a weary sigh.

Time passed. The house made the small, settling sounds that old houses do when the occupants are asleep. Snores of various pitch and volume could be heard from the bedrooms. Miss Forth's cat Cleopatra twitched her suddenly young-again paws as she hunted mice in her sleep.

And then,

Slightly sat up in the warm darkness of the kitchen, utterly wide awake. She felt very clever . . .

. . . and she was about to do something very foolish.

Chapter Nine:
Bright Ideas in the Dark

She had guessed the second meaning of the riddle and she was going, right now, to retrieve the real Dragonfish fossil, solve the case and save the day! It didn't even occur to her that waiting till morning might be a good idea.

She was going now. This minute.

Slightly's brain beat with excitement as she threw on her clothes.

We are not only bodies,
This we all know
In the house of bodies' final rest
I rest below.

We are not only bodies . . . souls, yes, but what's another word for souls? SPIRITS. And *bodies' final rest*? Not all bodies were buried in cemeteries or crypts. Some bodies – animal bodies, for example – ended up in museums! Like the Natural History Museum. Or one of the buildings *next* to the Natural History Museum. Like . . . THE SPIRIT BUILDING! *The house of bodies' final rest* was the Spirit Building! And at that moment Slightly would have happily bet anything in the world that the Natural History Museum's Spirit Building had a cellar – *I rest below* – and in that cellar she would find the Dragonfish!

And when that awful Snit comes to look for it in the morning, it won't be there any more, because I will have grabbed it and given it right back to Professor Appleword. So there!

She felt pretty smug about guessing *both* answers to the riddle! The question, *But why did Snit write the riddle like that in the first place?* tried to get her attention but she was having none of it. *I will not borrow trouble.* She let herself out of the front door, trotted down the steps – then paused.

Slightly had never been out alone at night before. She knew it could be dangerous. The great city of London never slept, and some of the people who were awake in the dark hours would do her harm as soon as look at her. But *some* folk were abroad with nothing more sinister on their minds than doing their normal work. And as Slightly hesitated in the shadows at the foot of the front steps, one of these nocturnal workers passed by. It was a carter, with a great, patient, shaggy-footed Shire horse and a wagon piled high with hay.

The cows in Hyde Park! thought Slightly and quick as a startled rabbit, she darted out, jumped up onto the back of the wagon and burrowed into the sweet-smelling hay. Had anyone seen her? She lay rigid, trying not to breathe, but the horse hadn't faltered in its slow, steady stride and the carter showed no signs of noticing he'd taken on a passenger.

The grass is getting used up, this time of year, she thought, *and the hay's been cut in the countryside. A good feed for the Hyde Park cows and a free ride for me!*

Slightly grinned to herself, wriggled a little to get comfortable and then lay still, on her back, looking up at each gas light as it passed overhead. Her heart had almost stopped its wild pounding, when the cart slowed perceptibly.

'Morning, Fred,' came a voice out of the darkness. There was a powerful smell that made Slightly guess this was the carter of a dung cart, travelling in the opposite direction. 'How's the missus? And that new baby of yours?'

'Beautiful, Sidney, just beautiful!' answered *her* carter. *So your name's Fred*, thought Slightly. *And you have a new baby!* 'Thanks for asking.'

The new voice sounded smiley. 'That's just grand. Tell her my Mary was asking after her. See you, Fred.'

'Aye. See you, Sidney.'

Slightly snuggled deeper into the fragrant hay and thought about Sidney and Fred making their journeys through the night while she and so many others slept. *Bring the hay in for one end*, she thought sleepily, *take the dung away from the other!* She started to giggle but it turned into a yawn instead and before she realised what was happening, she had fallen asleep . . .

. . . until something woke her again. The surface under the cart's wheels had changed. They had reached the Park! Slightly scrambled out of the hay, feeling bleary-eyed and panicky. She dangled her feet over the edge of the cart, then, before she could lose her courage, she jumped!

She landed on hands and knees in the dirt and though the breath was knocked out of her, she still managed to scurry into the shadow of the trees unnoticed. The cart trundled on. Slightly's heart hammering against her ribs, she peered about, frantically trying to orient herself – which is when she saw it. Rising up and glowing goldenly in the light of the gas lamps, she saw the Albert Memorial!

She knew the way to the Natural History Museum from here – she really did – it was along Queen's Gate, past the gardens of the Royal Horticultural Society to Cromwell Road. But nothing seemed the same at night. The moon was too far away to light the shadows between the gaslights and the wind was getting up, so that wisps of cloud kept obscuring its face.

Get going, Slightly, she scolded herself. She was finding it hard to breathe, but she set off as bravely as she could.

As she crept along by the Horticultural Gardens, strange scents came to her, some sweet, some horrible, but none familiar. The gardens seemed to stretch on forever and she began to think she'd made some mistake.

Should I go back? she thought. *Find the Memorial and try again?*

She'd almost decided to do that when . . . there it was, looming up in the darkness. She turned into Cromwell Road and found herself once again outside the magnificent front of the Natural History Museum.

She hurried along the pavement. The dead leaves still clinging to the trees whispered together in the night wind. Some of the posters for the Great China Exhibition had come loose from the railings and when one suddenly whipped off and flapped into her face, she couldn't help but scream.

But it seemed there was no one there to hear. The great wide street was empty. She knew London was home to thousands and thousands of souls, but at that moment she felt as if she were the last person left in the world.

She looked up at the terracotta statues perched on the walls of the Museum. The pterodactyls and wolf-like creatures she'd admired so much in daylight now seemed to be all teeth and odd angles in the flying moonlight. They seemed to glare at her and fidget hungrily, as if at any moment they were going to break free of the brickwork and swoop down for a closer look.

I shouldn't be here, she thought wildly to herself. *What was I thinking? I need to get away. I need to get home!*

For a moment she stood stock still, huddling against the cold railings, staring back the way she'd come. She realised she had no easy way to *get* home.

She'd come so far already, and her goal was practically in sight. She didn't have to *do* anything when she got there, and she was so close – it'd be foolish not to just go and take a *look* . . .

Slightly! she scolded herself. *Get a grip on yourself! What kind of behaviour is this for a detective?*

With all the willpower she could dig up, she pushed herself away from the railings and ran . . . towards Exhibition Road and the Spirit Building.

Almost there . . . almost there, she panted, and then – she *was* there. Right round the corner, out of sight, as if the beautiful main Museum were ashamed of it, stood the Spirit Building. *Sniffy Snit's Spirit House.* For the tiniest second, Slightly felt sorry for Professor Snit. But *only* for a second, for something else pushed the feeling right out of her head.

With a horrible jolt, she realised that she was no longer alone!

There was a shadow. It was small and silent and it was moving up to the door of the Spirit Building with all the quiet confidence of a soft-pawed cat. For a brief second a light flashed, as if from a shrouded lantern, and then darkness again. She couldn't see the shadow any more but she knew it was still there. What was it doing?

Slightly crept closer.

A stealthy clinking sound came to her ears, and another of those quick flashes of light showed that the shadow was indeed still there, working away at the lock. A tiny sigh of satisfaction was followed by a slight screech of hinges, and the shadow slipped inside.

Without pausing to *think first*, Slightly followed.

She was in a hallway. It was dark inside the Spirit Building except, there, under one of the doors, a strip of light showed. Slightly stared. She was filled with a deep conviction that whatever lay beyond that door would be immensely important. She forgot about the shadow she'd been following. She took two steps forward and –

Suddenly she was grabbed from behind by a pair of strong, thin arms. A foul-smelling pad of cloth was clamped over her mouth and nose. She twisted frantically, trying to get away.

'Oh no, you don't!' snickered her captor, and there was a gloating tone in that voice that she felt she knew, but the smell from the cloth was making her brain swim horribly. There was no way she could cry for help, but she struggled as hard as she could, kicking out wildly with her feet. She connected with a chair that clattered over with a loud noise – and suddenly the door to the outside world smashed back on its hinges and a man appeared.

It was Mr Thurgood!

'Unhand that child!' he bellowed and rushed forward to her rescue. So bravely did he rush, that he didn't see the chair until he'd tripped over it himself. The last thing Slightly saw as her consciousness faded away was Mr Thurgood falling fast, flailing, desperately trying to right himself as he cannoned past. And the last thing she heard was the unmistakable *doinnng* sound of Mr Thurgood's head banging hard into the brick wall . . .

Chapter Ten:
A Villainous Plot

When Slightly came to, she found herself unable to move. She was tied to a chair, her head was pounding and she had a horrible taste in her mouth. At that moment she had no idea what had happened or how she'd got there, but she had an overpowering sense that it was bad . . . *very* bad.

Where am I? For some reason it seemed important to work this out, though what Slightly really wanted to do was go to sleep. She squinted and blinked, trying to clear the fog out of her eyes.

First I was outside the Spirit Building, she thought laboriously, *and then I came inside and then . . .*

With a shudder she remembered the feel of those horribly strong arms pinning her and the suffocating smell.

There were boxes piled about, as if she were in some kind of storeroom. *Or a scientist's laboratory*, she thought, noticing equipment on a table. *Or . . .*

Here she shut her eyes tight again and shuddered. *I must be dreaming*, she thought. *This must be a nightmare.* But the pain in her head and the discomfort of her trussed-up limbs convinced her she was truly awake. She forced her eyes open . . .

. . . and forgot to breathe.

Everywhere she looked, there were racks of deathly white monstrosities, each trapped in jars of varying sizes, each swimming in some unknown caged sea.

Don't be afraid, she told herself. *Remember you're in the Spirit Building. They're just those wet specimens. They're safe. They're dead.*

But it was hard to believe herself.

She was surrounded by shelves of bleached, twisted fish . . . strange spiny creatures with long snouts . . . a snake as thin as a boot-lace and curled dozens of times to fit inside its jar. Some sort of octopus splayed its tentacles against the glass as if trying to escape. A baboon bared its teeth at her and wrung its frozen paws. And everywhere, unblinking eyes stared, fixing her with mad intensity and malice . . .

Unable to help herself, she whimpered out loud.

'Slightly?'

Which was when she realised she was not the only one there. Another captive was tied to a chair, secured back-to-back with hers, and that captive was –

'Mr Thurgood?!' she whispered.

'Oh child, thank goodness! I was so afraid you were dead!' cried Mr Thurgood, for it was indeed he. 'All I've been able to think of since I regained consciousness is how he must have killed you!'

'Killed me?!' Slightly shivered.

Mr Thurgood's voice was squeaky with relief. 'That brute Snit had no idea what he was doing. Chloroform can be very dangerous in the hands of an amateur, as I'm sure you remember from Chapter Six of my novel, when it was used with such bad effects by the villain Count Uglizador – I don't believe for a moment Snit was any more careful than the Count about measuring the dose. If that had happened to *you* . . . oh . . . I . . . I owe you an apology, dear child!'

'You don't!' exclaimed Slightly, but Mr Thurgood was still talking.

'I truly meant to rescue you, I truly did, well, I *am* the night-watchman, and instead all I managed was to knock myself out and . . .' Here his voice choked up and she could feel him slump dejectedly against his bonds.

But Slightly was having none of this. 'You are completely wrong, Mr Thurgood,' she said firmly. 'You definitely are. In my opinion it was positively heroic the way you burst in and stood up to the villain Snit . . .'

Slightly suddenly noticed, with horror, that Mr Thurgood had started to shake! For one awful moment she thought she'd made him cry.

'Oh I didn't mean, I mean, I . . .' she exclaimed, but then she realised something extraordinary. Mr Thurgood wasn't crying. He was laughing!

'The way I . . .' he spluttered. 'The way I *stood up* to him . . . oh my dear you're quite right. The *standing up* was excellent – it was the falling over that let me down . . . *Let me down* . . . Oh!' And he was off again, Slightly giggling uncontrollably along with him.

Under normal circumstances, none of this would have been all that funny but for some reason – perhaps the fact that they were tied up in a cellar awaiting a (most likely) unpleasant fate at the hands of a (probably) mad scientist – well, Slightly and Mr Thurgood laughed till they cried while all around them, white dead things looked on amazed.

At last, however, the captives calmed down again.

'Thank you, my dear,' said Mr Thurgood huskily. 'That was just what I needed. I feel much better now.'

Slightly smiled. 'Me too. I was wondering, though . . .'

'Yes? What were you wondering?'

'I was wondering what the characters in your book would make of a situation like ours. How would they go about escaping, for example?'

'Now that,' said Mr Thurgood, 'is a very good question and shows the clarity of thought I have always admired in you.'

'Thank you. And . . . ?' asked Slightly expectantly.

'Well, so far, I've mostly had another character come in and rescue them.' He paused for a moment. 'I don't suppose you told anyone – the police, for instance? or Miss Tonic? – where you were going when you left the house tonight?' There was a forlorn hope in his voice which Slightly hated to crush.

'No,' she said sadly. 'I didn't think to tell anybody. How about you?'

'No. There *is* only me doing the nightwatching.

It's expected I'll just get on and deal with things, though I realise now I never quite understood *how* I was supposed to deal. When I saw that the door to the Spirit Building was standing open and then I saw *you* – well, I just rushed in like an idiot. Stupid, stupid. Perhaps that's why my novel may never by published. I'm just too stupid to deserve it.' And, all the laughter gone, he moaned like a man in deep pain.

'I'm not surprised you're groaning,' said an unpleasant voice. 'I imagine you must each have quite a headache. Chloroform – which I used to overpower you, little girl – has that effect, and so does running headfirst into a brick wall – which is what your companion did so amusingly!'

It was Professor Octavian Snit.

The drip on the end of the Professor's long, white nose glistened in the light of the lantern he held, and his eyes were wild and strange. He gave a gloating laugh and wagged his finger in Slightly's face.

'But then, you have to expect consequences when you stick your noses into the work of a person of superior intellect,' he continued.

'You talk about *consequences*?' spluttered Mr Thurgood, furiously trying to squirm around to where he could see their captor. 'Don't you know that you might have *killed* this child, using chloroform on her in that, that, *uncontrolled* way? Is that the behaviour of a person of superior intellect?! I can't even imagine how you managed to be in possession of chloroform in the first place!'

'An *intelligent* man can acquire anything he sets his mind to!' drawled Snit. 'I wished to be prepared. After all, there was always the chance someone might have enough brains to work out the *real* answer to the riddle – not the ridiculously easy answer that would lead to the fake – any fool could have figured *that* out!'

Slightly remembered how proud of herself she'd been. *Any fool!* she thought bitterly. *Any fool – like me!*

'But that was a risk I was willing to take,' Snit continued. 'I don't expect you to understand. And I will admit to being surprised that anyone other than a professor was able to solve my double-riddle ... It's quite irritating, really. It was Appleword I wanted in that chair, not an interfering girl and a useless night-watchman!'

'She could have died!' repeated Mr Thurgood through gritted teeth.

Snit shrugged. 'I suppose. And if you hadn't so considerately made *yourself* unconscious, who knows what I might have had to do to *you*? I'm sure my friend Morbley would have found room for you, somewhere or other, if I'd miscalculated. He's very accommodating.' His eyes narrowed. 'I may make use of his services yet. I imagine that no one would believe any stories you might tell about me and this wretched fossil – not after it has been destroyed, of course. It would be your word against mine, and with no evidence to back you up . . .

'But what if you blab to Appleword and *he* tries to cause trouble? Even with a ruined reputation, he has friends in high places. *He* could still harm me. I *must* have my chance to fill the Museum with my beautiful specimens. I have my own jewel which should be given pride of place – something *worth* showing to the Queen . . . my *Magturpisres longissnomen.*'

Slightly watched with fascinated horror as Snit pulled a piece of lovely brocade off a jar on the table. He seemed to forget all about them as he gazed at it, turning the jar this way and that, so that the ghastly thing inside swung slowly round in the amber liquid, revealing strange bulges of dead white flesh, one staring eye and a distorted jaw forced open by rows of jagged teeth. It was probably the most appallingly hideous thing that Slightly had ever seen, but Professor Snit was murmuring, 'Beautiful . . . beautiful . . .'

And then he started to unscrew the lid. He unscrewed it, laid it gently to one side, leaned right down over the open jar and *inhaled deeply*!

Slightly knew it was stupid to draw attention to herself – she really did – but it was such a revolting sight . . .

'Yeuch!' she exclaimed.

Snit stiffened, and slowly replaced the lid. 'Hmm,' he said. 'This calls for more thought . . .' And he walked over and looked down at his captives with such an expression of cold calculation that both Slightly and Mr Thurgood gulped.

Then, with a disconcerting switch of mood, he started to smile . . .

He's mad! Slightly thought, trying not to panic. *What should we do?*

The answer came to her in a flash – keep him talking! If Slightly had learned anything from reading books, it was that villains liked to talk, and that while they were still talking, they weren't slitting your throat. And the longer they talked, the more likely they were to make A MISTAKE. Not just a little, no-problem sort of mistake but a BIG mistake which would shift the balance of power and, eventually, lead to the happy ending.

She had to keep him talking.

'Is it here?' she blurted. 'The Dragonfish fossil?'

'Of course it's here!' said Snit. 'Would I give a lying riddle? That wouldn't be fair at all. No, it's here. I couldn't leave it upstairs, in the main laboratory, in case anybody else started poking about. But no one comes down *here*. This is my own *special* laboratory.'

He walked to one of the shelves, moved some jars to one side, and there it was. The Dragonfish. He picked it up and circled round them, showing off his prize. It looked just like the terracotta copy, and yet, somehow, even more beautiful. For just a second, Slightly saw in her mind its story rewinding, back across the seas and overland to the Mogol's court, back to the peasant who found it when ploughing his field, back to the millennia of sleep under the weight of the ground and of a now-vanished sea above, back to the moment the Dragonfish lay itself down to sleep forever, back to a flash of wings in the sky –

Snit's voice wrenched her back horribly to the present. 'I'm sure you're desperate to know how I intend to destroy this troublesome lump of rock, this wretched fossil.' And he held the Dragonfish out at arm's length, as if it were something dirty or even contagious.

'Be careful!' cried Slightly. She couldn't help it.

Snit looked at her smugly and put it down.

'Well, yes,' he said. 'I *did* think of just dropping it, the way you dropped my terracotta fake! I must say, you did a *smashing* job! He-he.' When no one joined in laughing at his joke, he stopped tittering and continued smugly. 'The idea of tripping you up just came to me on the spot. For men of genius that's often the way, you know.'

'*You* tripped me!' exclaimed Slightly bitterly. 'I should have guessed.'

'Oh, now, you do the best you can, I'm sure,' said Snit with a sneer. At that moment, Slightly hated him utterly and she was sure it must show on her face, but he didn't seem to notice. Or perhaps he simply didn't care.

'I'll tell you what's wrong with repeating that method, though,' he continued. 'It leaves evidence. I don't want anyone coming across any left-over bits and getting any nasty suspicions. So no dropping it from a great height or bashing it with a sledgehammer. What I wanted was something that would destroy the Dragonfish utterly, completely, and forever. So that it would be as if it had never existed. What I wanted . . . was some kind of acid. And do you know what makes this even *more* delicious? I got a whole selection from Appleword's own laboratory!

That's right!' And he hugged himself, so great was his pleasure in his own cleverness. It made the drip on the end of his nose wobble, and his eyes looked madder than ever.

He was such a revolting sight that Slightly had to look away – and as she did so, she saw something that made her heart leap into her throat. The door to the stairs was moving! Ever so slowly, ever so gently, it was easing open. A shock of mud-coloured hair and a pair of bright brown eyes appeared for an instant in the gap, retreated, and then an entire boy slid through and scurried into hiding behind a rack of jars.

It was Matthew Bone! He must have been the shadowy figure she'd seen breaking into the building – the figure she'd followed. He must have been hiding upstairs somewhere all this time!

Mr Thurgood's words came into Slightly's mind. *'I mostly have another character come in and rescue them . . .'*

Oh no, she groaned silently. *Does it have to be HIM?!*

Slightly dragged her eyes back with an effort, but Snit was still talking about himself, and had noticed nothing.

'I took some pieces of rock as well, on which to try the acids. In the end, I came up with my own special recipe! It's so exciting to watch – you must see –' He'd put the Dragonfish down on the table, and now he took up a piece of limestone, put it in a metal dish, dribbled the liquid on and brought it up close for them to observe.

At once the stone began to bubble and hiss like a snake in terrible pain. There was an acrid stink that made their eyes sting. After less than a minute, Snit slopped some water over the rock and gleefully showed the result of his experiment to his captive audience.

The stone had been eaten away – even in such a short time! Slightly and Mr Thurgood were in no doubt that the Dragonfish would be completely destroyed if Snit used his acid on it.

'Please . . .' said Slightly, though she felt sick at pleading with such a man. 'Please don't do this . . .'

He wasn't listening.

'My timetable will need to be shifted forward,' he muttered, 'now that you two have stuck your noses in. I'd wanted Appleword here to see his precious fossil destroyed – and his future with it, of course – but now . . .'

Suddenly, Slightly stiffened in her chair.

'What was that?!' she gasped.

'What was what?' snarled Snit, turning round, staring suspiciously about.

'Oh . . .' said Slightly in a sly voice. 'Nothing . . . it was nothing.'

Snit loomed over her threateningly. 'Tell me this instant, or I'll . . .'

Slightly did her best to shrink away and blurted, 'Oh, please, don't hurt me – I'll tell you! I . . . I just thought I heard something. That's all. I'm sure I was mistaken.'

'Heard something? Where?' barked Snit.

'Up there! Upstairs! But it was probably nothing. No, I'm sure it was nothing . . .'

Snit narrowed his eyes. 'That's what you'd *like* me to think, isn't it? *You* think it's some sort of rescuer and you think you can make *me* think it's no such thing. Right. A few more minutes won't make any difference. I'll take a quick look around upstairs, just in case . . .' He picked up an oil lamp from the table and lit it with a safety match. At the doorway he paused and called back in a mocking voice, 'Now don't you two go anywhere!'

They could hear him sniggering at his own wit as he pulled the door to and started to climb the stairs.

Gotcha! crowed Slightly. *That was your BIG MISTAKE!*

Immediately, Matthew crawled out from his hiding place.

'Blimey!' he said. 'What a nutter! Now let's have a look at his knot work.' He had just bent to examine their bonds when a voice made him freeze in his tracks.

'I think not, boy,' it drawled.

Slightly, Matthew and Mr Thurgood gasped. It was Snit.

He must have gone out of the room and then just stood on the stairs, waiting . . .

'Did you really think I'd fall for your little act?' he sneered at her. He turned to Matthew. 'Fortunately, I have plenty of rope left – and my knot work, boy, is exceptional. As you are about to discover for yourself . . .'

CHAPTER ELEVEN:
Get Out!

Slightly's heart plummeted. All she'd managed to do with her cleverness was put Matthew in danger as well. But if she thought he would just tamely let himself be tied up, she could not have been more wrong! When Snit lunged at him, Matthew jinked over to the table and grabbed hold of the nearest jar, raising it, two-handed, above his head.

'I've got a . . .' he paused and lowered the jar to peer at the label, before hoisting it aloft again. 'I've got a great big ugly something with a long name and I'm not afraid to drop it!'

Slightly would not have thought that Octavian Snit's practically bone white face could have become any paler, but it did.

'No – no – not the *Magturpisres longissnomen!*' he gasped. 'You don't know what you're doing!'

'I think you'll find I always know *exactly* what I'm doing,' sniggered Matthew.

Idiot! moaned Slightly silently. *Think!* This really wasn't the time to be irritatingly overconfident. There'd been a mistake but it wasn't Snit's – it was Matthew's. Slightly could see that those skinny arms of his were already starting to shake – he'd chosen *far* too big and heavy a jar to kidnap.

'What's happening?' hissed Mr Thurgood frantically. The main action was now behind him, so that although Slightly had a ringside seat, *he* couldn't see what Matthew and Snit were up to. Slightly could feel him desperately trying to turn his head round 180 degrees. When a barn owl does this, it always looks so effortless, but even a potentially *great* novelist finds it more or less impossible. 'What's *happening*?'

In an agony of curiosity, Mr Thurgood tried to wrench his entire body round . . .

Slowly, inexorably, everything happened at once.

'NO!' cried Slightly as she felt the chairs begin to tilt sideways and flung herself wildly in the opposite direction in an attempt to stop them.

'NO!' cried Matthew as the *Magturpisres longissnomen* jar began to slip through his fingers.

'NO!' cried Snit as he threw himself forward to try to catch the jar.

There was an almighty crash as they all . . . failed.

Slightly and Mr Thurgood hit the floor so hard it knocked the breath out of them. Snit tripped and fell headlong, knocking over the lamp as he went. The jar smashed, causing the *Magturpisres longissnomen* to slither under the racks in a horrible imitation of life, as a wave of methylated alcohol splashed across the floor and started to spread fast, horrifyingly fast, until it reached the lamp that lay on its side –

– and exploded!

Fire! The flames hurtled up with an appalling, deafening roar. It was the most terrifying thing Slightly had ever seen. The sudden heat made her skin blister and her eyes felt as if they were being boiled. Her breath caught in her throat and her lungs burned. She tried to scream but she had no voice, she could only whimper like a cornered animal. Fear of fire, of pain, of death – she was close to fainting with it – when suddenly she became aware of hands wrenching at the ropes that held her. There was the sharp nick of a knife blade against her wrist, and then she was free!

'Get out!' a hoarse voice rasped in her ear. She was dragged upright. 'Go!' And someone pushed her away.

Bent double and coughing her heart out, Slightly staggered in the direction she'd been shoved, her eyes streaming, barely able to see through the stifling smoke. The door – she needed to find the door.

She slammed painfully into the edge of the table and as her hands grabbed at it, trying to steady herself, she felt a rough shape – stony – a pattern of some sort imprinted on its flat surface . . . Without any conscious thought, she caught up the shape, clutched it to her chest, and stumbled along the table to the left. Some tiny part of her brain remembered the layout of the room well enough to know that was the way she had to go . . . but it struggled to be heard above the crazed screams of *Run! Run anywhere! Just run!* that filled the rest of her mind.

She found the door, then lost precious seconds by forgetting which way it opened. She slammed it shut by mistake, then couldn't find the handle, then she couldn't make it turn one-handed. Finally, she scrabbled it open and fell through onto the stairs . . .

She dragged herself forward for what felt like hours, up the stairs and across the floor, wheezing and choking and hurting in every fibre, until somehow, she was at the door to the outside world.

It was shut.

And that was where she gave up. She couldn't get onto her feet. She couldn't open that door.

She tried to think of Granny and the others but she couldn't quite remember what they looked like any more. *I'll just sleep a little*, she thought. *I'm sure they won't mind . . .* She laid her head down. *Just like the Dragonfish*, she thought vaguely . . .

The next thing she was aware of was a rush of sweet, fresh, cold air. Strong hands grabbed hold of her and carried her outside.

'Here she is, Ma'am,' said an unfamiliar voice. 'She was just inside the door.'

'Thank you, Officer,' said a voice that was more familiar than any other in the whole world. It was Granny's voice and Granny's arms that took her over to a patch of grass and laid her down.

For a long time she could only cough and cough. Then, as the spasms finally eased, the tears started.

'Oh Granny,' Slightly wept uncontrollably. 'It was awful! I was so afraid – so afraid of the fire. I . . . I just ran! I left everything – everyone. Mr Thurgood! And

Matthew! And Snit! They're still down there!' She tried to stand up, but Granny was having none of it.

'They are most certainly not still down there,' she said firmly. 'Mr Thurgood and the boy dragged that good-for-nothing man out. The policemen who discovered me here on the grounds and was about to arrest me for "being where I shouldn't ought to be" is looking after them now. See? Just over there.'

'Then they're all right?'

'As all right as you, which is only so-so, in my opinion,' said Granny, but Slightly wasn't listening. She was too busy letting herself go and indulging in a crying jag.

'Oh, I'm such a coward!' she sniffled.

'You are no such thing,' snapped Granny. 'You are the most foolishly brave girl I have ever met. And how can you say you left everything when you are holding the Dragonfish fossil this very moment in your arms? Which, by the way, you really could put down. It's safe now. You rescued it, Slightly. You solved the case, and you saved the day!'

Slightly looked down at what she was holding so tightly. Soot-smudged but otherwise undamaged, the Dragonfish was, indeed, safe.

Slightly gave Granny a watery smile and let her take the fossil and set it down. As she did so, the

Fire Brigade came thundering up, smoke billowing from the chimney, the horses at full stretch. Shiny brass and silver helmets gleamed as the men rushed out the hoses, and the steam pump, groaning and hissing, began to work. It was exciting, but Slightly had trouble focusing on the bustling men. She tried to concentrate.

'Did you just say you were almost arrested? Really, Granny, I'm shocked!' Then she frowned and croaked, 'But that doesn't make sense . . . What are you doing here? How did you know this was where I was? I didn't even leave a note!'

'No,' said Granny sternly. 'You didn't, and I intend to have words with you on that subject, just as soon as you're fit to hear them. I'm here because I worked it out – the riddle – and got up, assuming you were still safe in bed, and came right over.'

'Did *you* leave a note?' asked Slightly, but Granny didn't answer. In fact Granny was beginning to behave very strangely indeed. She was going all hazy and wavy round the edges, then her voice sounded echoey and far away, and then . . .

Slightly fainted dead away.

Next morning when Slightly woke up, she took a deep breath and immediately wished she hadn't. Her face and hands were raw and sore, her eyes felt crusted and her chest burned. Granny was there and at once gave her something to drink that soothed her throat a little and made the room swim round.

I wonder if . . . ? she thought to herself drowsily. *I wonder what . . . ?*

But then she stopped wondering at all.

━ ✳ ━

It was a few days before Slightly was well enough, in Granny's opinion, to get any of her questions answered. To keep her from becoming frantic, they *had* assured her that no one had suffered lasting damage from the fire, though Professor Snit ended up with a very large lump on the back of his head.

'Apparently he panicked when the others tried to rescue him, and Mr Thurgood had to hit him over the head with a chair,' said Granny.

I wish I could have seen that! thought Slightly. Out loud, she asked, 'Where is Professor Snit now?'

'He's in hospital, with a police guard,' said Granny. 'And that's all I'm going to say about *him*.'

Mr Thurgood was in his own room, suffering

from smoke inhalation and some nasty burns, but there was no doubt that he would recover completely in time. Meantime, he was in excellent spirits and was using the enforced leisure to forge ahead with his novel.

And what of Matthew Bone?

After the fire, Granny had insisted on bringing him home. He'd been tucked up in the pallet bed in the kitchen, and Miss Forth had nursed him with a lot of enthusiasm. (This was out of genuine kindness and not *just* that she was keen to learn rhyming slang and backwards slang and thieves' language generally.) She treated him like a delicate flower and guarded him fiercely from any disturbance. The other boarders were reduced to bringing in food from the street vendors and eating in their bedrooms, so as not to disrupt the boy hero's rest.

Perhaps it was more care than he cared for, or perhaps he had business of his own to attend to. Whatever the reason, one morning, when Miss Forth came into the kitchen, she found that he was gone, along with some of the cutlery and a large cooked joint of beef!

'But . . .' said Slightly. She felt confused and hurt.

'I've no doubt we'll see him again,' said Granny. 'No doubt at all.'

And with that, Slightly had to be content.

She mended quickly. And the very first morning she was well enough to come down into the kitchen for breakfast was the morning the letter arrived . . .

The postman gave a double knock on the front door, and then another! He only did this for telegrams or letters of particular importance. Everyone listened hard as Granny hurried to the door and opened it.

'It's addressed to Miss Tonic and Miss Jones,' they heard him say. 'And I'm ever so curious to know what's in it . . .'

'Come in, come in,' said Granny.

The postman followed her into the kitchen, pulling off his cap and unbuttoning the red collar of his blue uniform for comfort. He laid a fine white envelope on the table. It had been beautifully addressed, with a blob of red wax sealing it.

'None of your modern glued envelopes,' he observed. 'This one's flash and no mistake!'

Granny slit the envelope open and handed the bit of deckle-edged card over to Slightly.

It was thick and creamy coloured with beautiful copperplate writing and fancy curlicues round the text. Slightly raced over the words so fast she didn't quite understand them at first. Then she read again, more slowly, and her face lit up with delight.

You are cordially invited to attend the
Private Viewing
and
Royal Unveiling
of
(among other exhibits)
The Mogol of Mongolia's
Dragonfish
(Dracopisciformia albertii)
This Monday
5:00 p.m

'And there's a P.S. as well — *We regret that the current state of Mr Thurgood's health means he will be unable to attend, but we look forward to his good recovery and return to his duties.*'

'Isn't that grand!' said the postman.

'Just as it should be!' said Mr Westerly.

'Yes,' said Mr Gentler. 'Richly deserved.'

And,

'What shall you wear?' said Miss Forth.

CHAPTER TWELVE:
At the Natural History Museum - By Invitation Only

Slightly and Granny arrived at the museum in good time and were ushered into the Central Hall by their friend the young guard. He had been tidied to within an inch of his life by someone, and was too nervous to do more than grin at them.

A red carpet had been laid from the front door through the Hall to the foot of the Main Stairs. There, the Dragonfish had been put into a new cabinet, specially prepared with a blue silk tent over it and a blue silk cord for Her Majesty to pull on for the unveiling. Every other cabinet and exhibit, from the giant tree slice to the sperm whale's vertebrae had been dusted and polished, brushed and buffed.

'It's all almost as magnificent as *we* are!' grinned Slightly and, indeed, both she and Granny were looking extremely presentable. Granny had on her best mauve damask dress and a tremendous hat, and the sleeves of Slightly's new blouse were so beautifully puffed that she felt she might not fit through the Museum's doors. (She did, of course, but they really were truly, deeply puffy.) Granny had brushed her hair for her till it shone, which was the most Slightly could expect from it.

As they stood to one side, watching the final fussing and fidgeting of the Museum staff, Slightly suddenly stiffened and grabbed Granny's arm.

'Granny!' she squeaked. 'I just realised – we haven't been keeping track!'

'Keeping track of what?'

'Of me losing my temper – we haven't kept track all week!'

Granny looked at her for a moment and then nodded. 'Well, then,' she said, 'let's just say you haven't lost your temper all week. Congratulations, Slightly!'

Slightly bobbed a cheeky curtsey and giggled.

'I hope you curtsey better than that when the Queen arrives,' began Granny but Slightly had just seen Professor Appleword and was waving enthusiastically at him.

The Professor's bald head shone. His cravat was tied to perfection and decorated with a pearl pin, and his fine frock coat was impeccable in every way. He was the perfect picture of a nervous, deliriously happy museum director.

'Dear Albert,' murmured Granny Tonic with a fond smile.

He caught sight of them and was just starting to cross over, when one of the attendants rushed up and whispered urgently in his ear.

Professor Appleword turned pale and hurried out of the Hall.

The invited spectators buzzed excitedly. This must be it! The Great Lady must be near!

Slightly's heart was pounding against her new blouse so hard the fabric rustled.

But then something truly awful happened.

The Queen of the United Kingdom of Great Britain and Ireland, Empress of India, Defender of the Faith, came into the Central Hall. And as her monarch walked carefully along the red carpet, one word rose inexorably into Slightly's mind.

Dumpling.

Not for worlds would Slightly Jones have allowed a word of criticism of her monarch to be uttered in her presence. Far less would she have ever done so herself. But the inescapable fact was that Queen Victoria was very short and very round, and the black dress that she wore was not designed to hide either of those things. She really *did* look like an overdone dumpling.

Slightly swallowed hard. *I am a traitor!* she thought.

But then something wonderful happened.

Queen Victoria had turned to the crowd and was giving a dignified wave, when her eyes lit on Slightly. She walked off the carpet and right over to her.

Slightly stopped breathing.

'What lovely hair!' said the Queen, touching Slightly's hated red curls gently with a hand gloved in black lace. 'How lucky you are, my dear!'

And then she smiled. Her face lit up, and at once Slightly was filled to the brim with the belief that this was the most charming monarch a nation could have. Her Queen!

She dropped a curtsey and smiled back. 'Thank you, Your Majesty,' whispered Slightly Jones.

Then, under the benign eye of Mr Darwin, Queen

Victoria did her duty by her country, and pulled the silken cord . . .

'Ooooh!' said the Queen.

'Ooooh!' echoed the crowd.

The cloth fluttered to the floor without getting stuck on anything. The Dragonfish – the *real* Dragonfish, resting in its beautiful Chinese box – was revealed to all.

❧

The Queen viewed the other exhibits in Professor Appleword's company, listening courteously to his explanations of the black panther and the white wallaby, the owl's winter plumage and the variations of crows and goldfinch. She was suitably impressed by the size of the sperm whale's mighty skeleton, and marvelled at the age rings on the great sequoia slice. Then, all too soon, she left. No one else wished to, however. They all wanted to mingle and gossip and exclaim over the Viewing and the Queen and the Dragonfish and the dramatic events of the last week.

Professor Appleword could barely keep his feet on the ground.

'This has been quite a time for you, Albert,' said Granny.

'It has, Lily, it has indeed!' he replied.

Then Granny must have noticed that Slightly's ears were flapping and abruptly changed the subject.

'And what of the man Snit?' she asked.

'He is almost well enough to leave the hospital,' replied the Professor solemnly.

'What will happen to him then?' asked Slightly. She honestly didn't know what answer she wanted to hear. Part of her wanted him to be punished for what he'd done. But now that it was over, and they were all safe, and Professor Appleword and Mr Thurgood both had their jobs back – well, part of her wanted the bad things to be over for Snit, too.

She looked at Professor Appleword, and wondered what *he* wanted.

'Octavian Snit will be sent to Scotland,' said the Professor. 'There is a Home for the Educated and Unbalanced near Aberdeen where he will be helped to recover from his unfortunate obsession. Between you and me, I think it is quite possible he may have been sniffing the spirits in which his specimens were stored – and that can't have been good for him.'

Slightly shuddered. She knew all too well that this was the truth.

'I have every hope,' the Professor continued, 'that he will be able to leave the events of the last while behind him, and apply his enthusiasm to another, less damaging, area of science. The world has so many wonderful things to be discovered, don't you think? And knowledge – well, it can heal most anything.' He looked straight at Slightly and added, 'Don't you agree?'

Slightly paused for a moment to consider. Did she agree? She thought hard, and then a smile spread slowly across her face.

'Yes, Professor Appleword,' she said. 'I do.'

By the time Professor Appleword put them into a hansom cab, both Granny and Slightly were too tired to do more than smile contentedly at each other. All the things they wanted to say would have to wait for another day. By the time they arrived home, it was past the entire household's bedtimes, but when Granny unlocked the front door (quietly, so as not to disturb anyone) they became aware that nobody was in bed at all. A hum of voices came from the kitchen . . .

'Have you all waited up for us?' asked Granny, entering the room with a smile.

'Yes, was it wonderful?'

'Did you really see the Queen?'

'What was it like?'

They were all there, seated around the big oak table – Miss Forth, Mr Thurgood (up, briefly, for the first time), Mr Westerly, Mr Gentler and . . .

. . . *another* Mr Gentler!

Granny and Slightly stared. The likeness was very clear.

'This is my dear brother, John,' explained their Mr Gentler. 'He's come all the way from Scotland – from Glasgow – on the train, because he's in terrible trouble.'

'I've no one to turn to, no one I can trust,' said the second Mr Gentler.

He sounds much more Scottish than our Mr Gentler, thought Slightly.

'What trouble are you in, Mr, er, John?' asked Granny, settling herself at the table to listen. Slightly leaned against her, as there were no chairs left, and listened to Mr Gentler's brother's dilemma . . .

No matter how tired and sleepy she'd been a moment ago, Slightly was wide awake now! It was a story of ghosts and ghouls and warnings from beyond the grave, of inexplicable thefts, of midnight beasts and a one-legged mystery. By the time he was finished, Slightly wasn't leaning any more. She was standing straight up and her eyes flashed with excitement.

'I'm at my wits' end,' said Mr Gentler's brother as bravely as he could, though his voice quavered a little. 'I don't know what to do!'

'Do nothing!' cried Slightly Jones. 'We'll take the case!'

TO BE CONTINUED IN
The Case of the Glasgow Ghoul

Discover
some fascinating
facts about Victorian
London...

Did you know...

... what Victorians used instead of texting?

During the time that Slightly and Granny lived in London, there were up to twelve postal deliveries a day. A note sent from one side of the city was expected to reach the other side only a couple of hours later – not quite instantaneous, but not bad.

... what the Muffin Man had on his head?

The Muffin Man was a door-to-door crumpet salesman with a tray on his head. There's a song about him too:

> Oh, do you know the muffin man,
> The muffin man, the muffin man,
> Oh, do you know the muffin man,
> That lives on Drury Lane?

Drury Lane is a street in London. If Slightly went there, then she would see the very first Sainsburys, opened in 1869.

... how to get a job in the Fire Brigade?

'Candidates for appointment must be seamen; they should be under the age of 25, must measure not less than 37 inches round the chest, and are generally preferred at least 5 feet 5 inches in height. They must be men of general intelligence, and able to read and write; and they have to produce certificates of birth and testimonials as to character, service etc. Each man has to prove his strength by raising a fire escape single handed with the tackle reversed.'

... how to behave on a London omnibus?

Travelling by omnibus in London was not always a pleasant experience. Buses were often crowded and had dirty straw on the floor. During many times of the day journeys were extremely slow on London's busy streets.

On 30 January 1836, *The Times* newspaper published a set of instructions for its readers, which were intended to make omnibus travel more enjoyable. Passengers on public transport could do worse than follow these rules today!

Omnibus Law

1. Keep your feet off the seats.

2. Do not get into a snug corner yourself and then open the windows to admit a North-wester upon the neck of your neighbour.

3. Have your money ready when you desire to alight. If your time is not valuable, that of others may be.

4. Do not impose on the conductor the necessity of finding you change: he is not a banker.

5. Sit with your limbs straight, and do not with your legs describe an angle of 45, thereby occupying the room of two persons.

6. Do not spit on the straw. You are not in a hogsty but in an omnibus travelling in a country which boasts of its refinement Behave respectfully to females and put not an unprotected lass to the blush, because she cannot escape from your brutality.

7. If you bring a dog, let him be small and be confined by a string.

8. Do not introduce large parcels – an omnibus is not a van.

9. Reserve bickerings and disputes for the open field. The sound of your own voice may be music to your own ears – not so, perhaps, to those of your companions.

London Quiz

Test your knowledge of Victorian and modern-day London with these questions . . .

Why would Morbley, Granny and Slightly have trouble getting into the crypt of All Souls' Church in the 1890s? What's under there now?

The church was built by the architect John Nash. His design was not usual for the time – and he got some pretty negative reactions to it!

A reviewer for *The Mirror* of Literature, Amusement, and Instruction August 2, 1828, said: "To our eye, the church itself, apart from the tower, (for such it almost is) is perhaps, one of the most miserable structures in the metropolis."

In March 1824, in the House of Commons, an MP described All Souls' as a "deplorable and horrible object". And in the press, a cartoon showed poor old Nash speared on the spire! The article called the church "an extinguisher on a flat candlestick".

Why don't you have a look at a picture of the church and make up your own mind – is it utterly ugly or as beautiful as John Nash wanted it to be?

If you visit the Natural History Museum today can you find the following?

* Slightly's favourite terracotta decorations (there are two kangaroos outside and two fox panels inside)
* The 'horrible great sloth'
* A wet specimen
* There's no part-dragon part-fish fossil (and there never has been!), but can you find an archaeopteryx? It's part something, part something else – what? Why is it such an important fossil?
* The display board on Mary Anning - Fossil Finder

Can you guess what *Magturpisres longissnomen* means in English?

Do you know what these words (which are part of Matthew Bone's Victorian thieves' slang) mean:

wipe	moniker
rozzers	nab
geezer	scarper
slavey	nick
rum fogle	needful

To find the answers to these questions and learn more about her other books, visit the author's website:

www.joanlennon.co.uk

THE ELEVENTH ORPHAN
by Joan Lingard

Mr and Mrs Bigsby of the Pig and Whistle,
Stoke Newington already look after ten children.
When Constable O'Dowd bring them an eleventh
orphan he found on the streets, Ma Bigsby is
reluctant to take her.

But there's something about Elfie, it's 1900, the first
day of a new century and Ma loves a mystery. Just
why does Elfie possess a little watercolour of
the Pig and Whistle?

As the mystery unfolds, Elfie's world will
change completely.

Shortlisted for the Royal Mail Awards

CHILDREN OF WINTER
by Berlie Doherty

Out walking, deep in the Derbyshire hills, Catherine and her family are forced to take shelter from a sudden storm in an old barn.

It all seems strangely familiar to Catherine. As the torchlight dims, shadows of the past crowd in, memories of a time hundreds of years ago, when three children took refuge in a barn, not from a storm, but from a terrible plague . . .

This gripping and haunting adventure is inspired by the true story of the village of Eyam which in 1665 cut itself off from the rest of Derbyshire, so that no other village would catch the Plague.

"Vividly and sensitively realised" GUARDIAN

You can find out more about other
exciting Catnip books by visiting:

www.catnippublishing.co.uk